The Ghosts of Tara

An Irish Mystery

Frances Powell

Other novels by Frances Powell

The Bodyguard

Mystery of White Horse Lake: An Irish Mystery

The Chief Cameron Fergus Mystery Series:

> *Lady of the Wye*

> *Murder in the Royal Forest of Dean*

A Ballysea Mystery Series:

> *The O'Brien*

> *A Bad Wind Blowing*

> *The O'Brien: The Untold Story*

> *A Ballysea Christmas*

Cover Design by: Jo Stallings

This book is dedicated to my grandson, Aidan Patrick Bange, who first told me of those things which can only be seen and heard by those willing to look and listen.

To my dear friend Theresa —
Thank you so much
for all your kind words
and your amazing
photos!
Love,
Fran

Table of Contents

Chapter 1

I always knew they were there, hiding under my bed or in the closet, peering out from the shadows... always there...always lurking. They never spoke and I never saw them, but I always felt their presence.

Of course, no one believed me. Why should they? To grown-ups, I was just that weird kid with the overactive imagination, most likely brought on by where I lived, they would whisper behind their hands. Our neighbors out back never bothered me like they did some people. It wasn't like they were bad neighbors, like the noisy people next door. As a matter of fact, they were dead-quiet. Well, they would be, wouldn't they? Dead people usually are and the cemetery behind my house was overrun with dead people.

After fifteen years, I had actually grown accustomed to their presence in my bedroom. At least my invisible roommates didn't have the ability to bully me like the kids at school. OK, I'll admit I don't exactly look like most of the other kids; but really, what is this thing people seem to have about freckles and red hair? I'm not carrot head, or ginger, I'm just plain Lucy Burke. It's like we're things left behind by an alien visitation or something. At least, when I got tired of my invisible company, all I had to do was simply walk out of the room and shut the door. My invisible roommates never strayed past my bedroom door. Don't ask me why, because I have absolutely no idea, unless they didn't like the bickering that always seemed to go on in the rest of the house. Short of running away from home and having to live on the streets, there didn't seem anyway of escaping the bullying at school.

Sometime after my fifteenth birthday, things got worse at my house and I began spending more and more time in my bedroom to avoid the no-holds-barred, all-out arguments between Mom and Dad. I found myself spending most of my spare time after school playing online video games with strangers who would never know my true identity but only my online persona. I began to find myself slowly sinking into the imaginary worlds where my games took me, anything to escape reality.

I'm not sure what changed between my parents, but three weeks before my sixteenth birthday, they suddenly announced I was going to spend a year in Ireland with the grandmother I'd never met, so they could sort out the details of their separation. I was finally going to escape the bullying at school, the invisible presence in my bedroom and the arguments at home without having to live on the streets. It seemed like a win-win to me. Or was it?

Chapter 2

A week later, I was being driven south on Interstate 95 from our home in Catonsville to Dulles International Airport to board my Aer Lingus flight. Traffic, as usual, came to a standstill once we exited onto the Washington Beltway that would take us towards the airport. Within ten minutes, Mom was clutching the steering wheel, white-knuckled and ranting and raving about the traffic and cussing out my father for not having the decency to take the time to drive us to the airport. As soon as she started, I fumbled into my backpack and pulled out my headphones and turned up the volume on my favorite station. It really didn't bother me that Dad didn't come to see me off. In all reality, he hadn't spent much time with me the last year anyhow. Dad wasn't what you would call a "hands-on" father like some you see on television. He was either at work or playing golf with his friends. I'm sure that was a large part of the problem between my parents and sometimes I felt that everything that was wrong between them was my fault. Maybe, he avoided being at home because I was there.

We arrived at the airport just in time for Mom to give me a hurried hug and kiss before my flight was called for boarding. After a seemingly endless night of watching the onboard movies and trying to get my 5'7" body comfortable in the cramped seats, the cabin lights flickered on and the cabin crew hurriedly served us some cold, stale tasting blueberry muffins and weak coffee before preparing for landing. I was so happy to be out of the cramped airplane that even the long wait standing in line at Passport Control felt like a treat to me.

When it was my turn at the counter, I was greeted with, "Welcome home Miss," despite my blue American passport. I started to correct him, and then realized that he was smiling as he stared at my red hair and freckles, so I just smiled. Perhaps here in Ireland, I could finally escape being called "ginger."'

Following the crowd, I soon found myself standing around the luggage carousel with the rest of my fellow passengers impatiently waiting for our luggage to slide by. After grabbing my case off the carousel, I followed the crowd and found myself in the arrivals area. Mom had told me to look for a man holding up a sign with my name written on it. He was to drive me to where my grandmother lived an hour or so outside Dublin.

As I walked up and down looking at the seemingly endless line of men of all shapes and sizes holding up signs, I saw him. He was a tall man about my father's age, dressed casually, unlike all the other suited men, As soon as he saw me, he smiled and walked over, "Welcome to Ireland, Miss Lucy. If you give me your luggage and follow me, we'll be on our way."

Just nodding and forcing a tired smile, I followed until I stopped dead. Coffee! I smelled coffee and at this very moment, I would sell my soul for a strong, hot cup of coffee.

Running up and grabbing my driver by his jacket sleeve, I pleaded, "Could we just stop long enough for coffee? That coffee they gave me on the plane was disgusting."

"Of course, have a seat and stay with your luggage and I'll get it for you. What kind would you like Americana, Latte, or Cappuccino?"

"Cappuccino, please with lots of sugar," as I reached into my purse and began fumbling around for the money Mom had made sure to give me.

"Put your money away, Miss Lucy. I have this, my treat."

Before I could object, he was gone. Suddenly remembering I'd promised to call Mom, I grabbed my phone and punched the numbers in. It rang the full eight times before the answering machine picked up so I hung up without leaving a message.

"Guess, no one is really worried about whether I got here safe and sound," I muttered under my breath.

"What's this about safe and sound, Miss Lucy?"

I hadn't realized my driver had returned with our drinks and packets of sugar and now stood hoovering over me like a mother hen.

"Nothing really, thanks for the coffee," as I lifted the sweet, frothy drink to my lips and drank.

I had almost finished when he began to smile and motioned to the area above my upper lip before passing me a napkin to wipe off my newly acquired mustache.

We finished our drinks in silence and then we were off weaving our way through the crowded terminal to the parking lot and our car. We had been driving through the lush, green, sheep-filled countryside for a little over an hour when, despite the caffeine delivered to my veins, my eyelids began to feel heavy and my eyes drifted shut, as I finally succumbed to the sleep that had eluded me on the overnight flight.

When I slowly opened my eyes as the car finally came to a stop the massive gray, stone building in front of me was still bathed in the morning mist, as the sun had just begun to creep over the horizon. Rubbing the sleep from my eyes, my mouth fell open at the sheer size of the place. It was massive! It was bigger than even the White House. Surely, this wasn't my grandmother's house.

Gathering up all my courage, I asked the driver, who until now had remained silent during the drive, "Does my grandmother work here?"

Looking into the rear view mirror, he raised his eyebrows and peered at me questioningly from under the brim of his cap, "Work?"

"Yes, work," I repeated.

"Well, in a manner of speaking, I suppose she does. It's a lot of work keeping a big place like this running smoothly."

Just nodding, my brain now formed an image of my aged grandmother employed as the housekeeper to the wealthy owners and wondered what my life would be like here. I had watched a lot of period dramas and I could just picture my grandmother still dressed in black mourning for my grandfather, who had been dead these past twenty years, performing all types of drudgery.

I was so lost in my thoughts I hadn't even noticed the driver had been patiently standing beside the car, holding the door open for me. Grabbing my backpack, I climbed out of the car and muttered a subdued, "thank you."

"Welcome, young miss. I'll just get your bag from the boot and I'll take you to meet your grandmother."

"The boot?"

"Yes, Miss. I believe you Americans call it the trunk."

The driver, who I later discovered was named Malcom Collier, carried my bags up the front steps and leaving them there, turned and said, "This time of day, your grandmother will likely be in the stables. Follow me, Miss."

'Oh damn, this is worse than I thought. It's barely the crack of dawn and they have the poor old woman mucking out the stables. What has Mother got me into? How could she allow her own mother to live this way?' I thought as I followed Mr. Collier across the cobbled courtyard to what I could only assume, from the smell permeating the still morning air, was the stables.

As we entered the stable, Mr. Collier called out, "Mrs. Lacy, are you here?"

"Over here," came the soft, lilting response.

I held my breath, squared my shoulders, and tried to compose myself as I prepared for the first glimpse of what I feared was my long-suffering grandmother. What I saw next left my mouth gaping wide, like a fish that had just been caught on a hook. Before me brightly smiling was a woman in her 60's with fashionably cut, short, silver hair, dressed in form-fitting cream-colored riding jodhpurs, brushing down a beautiful chestnut horse.

Dropping the brush, the woman came over and placing a hand on each of my forearms, looked me up and down and smiled saying, "Welcome to Tara, Lucy."

OK, I'd read *Gone with the Wind* in school and I knew in an instant that I wasn't in Georgia anymore. Matter of fact, I was in a completely foreign land about to be hugged by a complete stranger claiming to be my grandmother.

"You have the look of your great-great grandmother. Now give your grandmother a hug."

I was suddenly being pulled into the arms of this stranger who I was now expected to call Grandmother. Releasing me from her hold, she turned her attention back to the horse, "This is Dailtín. Isn't he lovely? Do you ride, child?"

Bristling at being called a child, after all I'll be sixteen in just a few days; I simply shook my head in response

"Well then, we'll soon remedy that. Your mother could ride when she was just a wee child, you know," she replied whimsically with a sudden far-away look in her eyes. Shaking her head, she re-focused her attention on me and continued, "You must be hungry and tired after your long flight. Let's get you into the house and get you settled, shall we?"

I was neither tired, after just waking from a nap, nor overly hungry but was curious to see where I was to live.

A sudden movement in the shadows of the stall had me thinking, 'good grief, they've followed me here' until a boy about my age stepped from the shadows and took the reins of Dailtín, as my grandmother prepared to leave. Catching me staring at the boy, Grandmother quickly introduced us, "Lucy, this young man is Cieran. Cieran is in charge of the stables when he's not at school. His father, Mr. Collier, the gentleman who picked you up from the airport, is the estate manager. They live here on the estate, so I'm sure you'll be seeing a lot of each other."

The boy just nodded in my direction, quickly lowered his eyes and was gone, leading Dailtín away, but not before I noticed he had the most incredible blue eyes, in sharp contrast to his raven black hair. He was probably the most gorgeous boy I'd ever seen. Hmmm…maybe things wouldn't be so boring here after all. I was still standing there staring after his retreating figure when my grandmother's voice woke me from my daydreaming.

"Come along Lucy, let's get you settled and then we can have some tea and you can tell me all the news from home."

With my backpack slung over one shoulder, I followed my newly-acquired grandmother back across the cobbled courtyard up the steps through the massive, imposing doors. Once inside, my eyes were immediately drawn to the biggest staircase I'd ever seen. Now, I had seen a lot of big houses on television but nothing prepared me for the sheer grandeur of this.

While I stood there gaping, Grandmother, as if reading my mind, gently said, "I had the same reaction as you when I came here as a bride forty years ago. It does rather take one's breath away, doesn't it? Now, let's go have that tea and you can tell me what's really going on with your mother and father."

Opening the first door off the huge entry hall, she turned and gazed into my eyes, "I'm sure your mother hasn't told me the whole story but I know things must be very uncomfortable for her to send you to me."

The room was huge with almost floor to ceiling windows that overlooked the beautifully manicured grounds beyond. The wide oak floors were covered with Persian rugs and sofas and arm chairs filled the room giving it a cozy appearance despite its size. A round mahogany serving table sat in front of the ornate fireplace, flanked by two cream colored, over-stuffed Queen Anne arm chairs.

Entering the room, Grandmother made right for what I assumed was her chair and waved her hand towards the chair opposite. I must have looked like the canary that had been cornered by the house cat as I sat there perched on the edge of the chair, staring down at my feet.

A tray set with tea and an assortment of cakes and the smallest sandwiches I had ever seen lay waiting on a table in front of the fireplace. As she poured the tea, I asked with lowered eyes, "Why do you say that?"

Ignoring my question, Grandmother began pointing at each tiny sandwich and describing their contents, there were egg salad, ham and cheese, and of all things, cucumber and creamed cheese. Maybe, the strange combination was thrown together just in case I was a vegetarian. In any case, I went right for the cakes and ignored the tiny, finger sandwiches.

Putting the teapot down, Grandmother reached over and taking one of my hands in hers asked, "Dear child, you are my only grandchild, haven't you ever wondered why you never visited me here before?"

Feeling slightly embarrassed, I figured the best plan of action was to tell the truth, so I just blurted out, "I never even knew I had a grandmother until two weeks ago."

Solemnly nodding, Grandmother picked up the tea pot and finished filling the cups before continuing, "I thought as much. Your mother and I fell out when she left with your father. You see, she was engaged to a local young solicitor and the wedding was all planned and then one day she met your father and within two weeks told me she was going away with him. Not getting married, mind you, just going to America to live with him.

We argued and I hadn't heard a word from her until a few weeks ago when she called and asked if you could come stay here at Tara for a while."

I frequently heard my father call my mother hard-headed and unforgiving but I had to admit, even as stubborn as I admitted to being, I could never hold a grudge against my own mother for seventeen years.

Shifting uncomfortably in my chair, I stared down at the remains of my tea and replied, "I think Mom and Dad are finally getting a divorce."

Nodding, grandmother grew silent and stared past me in the direction of the fireplace behind where I sat. Sighing deeply as she pointed to the portrait that hung above it, she hesitated as if measuring every word, "I was afraid of that. They were never really compatible and that was my only objection to them being together. Your mother was strong-will and headstrong and unfortunately I spoiled her terribly. Personally, I found your father to be quite a nice man and very charming, extremely talented, too."

Staring up at the portrait, I could hardly believe the woman, dressed in a beautiful ball gown and smiling down from there was my mother.

"She looks so different. I hardly recognize her as my mother."

"Why do you say that? Has she changed that much?"

Turning my head to the side and staring at the painting, it finally struck me, "No, she hasn't really changed that much, but I've never seen my mother smile like that. She seems so alive and happy."

Still gazing up at her daughter's portrait, Grandmother just smiled and said, "Yes, I believe she was never happier than the day that portrait was painted."

"Really, why was that?"

Patting my hand, Grandmother sighed as she said, "Well, my dear Lucy, I'm afraid that is something you must ask your mother when you speak to her. It's not my story to tell."

The rest of the day passed very quickly as Grandmother and I chatted about life in America and what I could expect from my move to Ireland and before I knew it dinner had come and gone and it was time for bed.

As was my nightly habit, I slid my laptop from my backpack and attempted to logon to the internet. Nothing…absolutely nothing. It never dawned on me that when I moved to Ireland I would not only be disconnected from my dysfunctional family in America but my make-believe cyber friends, too. Dammit, how am I ever going to survive a year without the internet? .

Chapter 3

I must have been more tired than I realized because the first thing I was conscious of the next morning was Grandmother pulling open the heavy, rose-colored draperies and bright sunlight flooding into my bedroom.

"Time to wake-up, sleepy head. Did you sleep well?"

Struggling to sit up in the over-sized bed, I yawned widely and rubbed the sleep from my eyes, "Actually, I haven't slept so well in a long time."

"Aye, it must be the fresh Irish air. Breakfast will be ready in fifteen minutes, I usually eat quite early in the kitchen but I thought it would be nice if we could start the day off together. See you downstairs in the dining room." She was quickly gone as she turned and headed to the bedroom door pulling it shut behind her.

Climbing out of bed, I sat there for a few minutes thinking to myself, 'It's not the fresh Irish air that gave me such a peaceful sleep. It's the quiet here, without the noise caused by my uninvited bedroom guests back home.' Stretching and widely yawning, despite my good night's sleep, my eyes scanned the room which my grandmother referred to as my bedchamber. At home, people might have called it a master suite, but one on steroids. The mahogany four-poster bed that I was barely able to drag myself out of was big enough for a family of four. The crisp white sheets were made of the finest Egyptian cotton topped with a soft, rose-colored down cover of what must have been stuffed with the finest of goose down. Patting the bed as if it was my loyal hound, I finally dragged myself out of bed and padded barefoot across the thickly padded carpet into the bathroom. For being such an old house, I was surprised at the beautifully updated bathroom which included a large walk-in shower with a waterfall showerhead alongside an antique claw-foot soaking tub. I ran my hand longingly around the smooth rim of the luxurious tub and mentally promised myself that I would be back soon for a long soak, but this morning there was no time. It didn't take me long to have a quick shower, dress and head down the staircase to join Grandmother for breakfast.

I was almost to the bottom of the staircase when I saw them. Lying there and blocking my progress was two of the biggest, hairy beasts I'd ever seen. Their eyes were barely visible through the wiry hair that hung down over them. As I took one more cautious step, they rose to their feet and continued to stare at me, heads lowered and front legs spread, as if deciding what should be done about this intruder in their house. I had no other choice but to try to keep my hands from shaking and sound calm. "Grandmother, can you help me?"

Hurrying into the center hall from the dining room, Grandmother first looked at my gaping mouth and wide eyes and then hands on her hips, frowned at the beasts blocking my progress, "Lancelot, Guinevere, outside, now", she firmly commanded as she pointed to the open front door.

As the two hounds, long tails tucked between their legs, slowly ambled out the door, turning only once to stare back at us, Grandmother reached up and took my hand, "Sorry if they startled you, love. I should have warned you about them. They're quite harmless, just curious. I'll take you out and properly introduce you after breakfast."

It wasn't a cold morning but a fire was lit in the dining room. I found out later that even with the central heating that these big rooms with such high ceilings were often a bit chilly in the morning. For such a large room though it was bright and cozy with the morning sun streaming through the nine foot tall windows that looked out over the gardens. After filling my plate with the delicious smelling offerings from the silver, covered dishes on the sideboard, I sat down opposite Grandmother as she poured me a cup of tea.

"Did you sleep well, my dear?" she asked again.

"Yes, that bed is really comfortable and the room is beautiful, but huge. I could fit four of my bedrooms at home into that one."

"I'm glad you felt at home there. It was your mother's room. Virtually nothing has been changed in it since she left, except the bathroom. All the bathrooms in the house were updated just last year. They really were serviceable and it was quite an expense but you see, I stayed in a posh hotel in Dublin and fell in love with the waterfall shower in the bathroom so I just had to have them installed in all the bathrooms."

Looking around the ornate dining room with its expensive furniture and antique paintings, I thought, 'Well, that must have been some hotel if it was fancier than Tara', but just replied, "Its perfect, Grandmother."

Grandmother just smiled and nodded as she raised her cup to her lips and sipped her tea. I couldn't help but notice while my plate was piled high with sausage, potatoes, eggs and toast that Grandmother's plate held just two pieces of toast and a small cup of fruit. I guess she must have noticed me staring and said, "I eat light these days, Lucy. When you get old like me, your appetite diminishes and then us ladies have to look after our figures. When I was your age, I actually ate twice as much for breakfast as what you have on your plate right now."

I glanced over at the youthful looking woman seated opposite me and thought, 'Well, whatever she's doing, it's sure working because she looks great for someone her age. Except for the silver hair, she didn't look much older than Mother.'

"What would you like to do today?" she asked lifting a piece of toast to her mouth.

"I was hoping you would have time to show me around the house. I hate to admit it but I almost got lost just coming downstairs from my bedroom to here."

"Of course, I'll be happy to and don't feel bad, Lucy, it was a good month before I could find my way around when I first came here."

After breakfast, I was taken on a tour of the house as Grandmother pointed at the many portraits hanging up the grand staircase. As we reached the top, she stopped and whispered, "Quite incredible."

Gazing up at the portrait of a woman dressed in a beautiful emerald-green gown I gasped out loud. It was like I was looking into a mirror...the same long, red hair, the same green eyes, and the same turned-up nose. Now, I understood, why my grandmother said that I had the look of my great-great grandmother. That was an understatement. We could have been twins!

After a tour of the few upstairs rooms that were not closed off, we ventured out the front door where Lancelot and Guinevere were lying like statues, one on either side on the massive door. Lumbering to their feet at Grandmother's approach, the massive beasts began to gently nuzzle her hands until she finally reached into her jacket pocket and handed them a couple treats.

As they accepted their treats, Grandmother spoke gently to them in a strange, melodic language which I later got to know as Gaelic before turning to me, "Lancelot and Guinevere are Irish Wolfhounds and their breed is as old as Ireland itself. They were once war dogs that accompanied their masters into battle and would protect them with their lives if they were ever unseated from their horse. They are also credited with ridding Ireland of wolves. They are really gentle giants now but I sleep very easy at night knowing that they are on guard. As you found out this morning, no one gets past them."

The morning mist had faded and for the first time I could see Tara in all its brilliance, bathed in bright sunlight. It was simply magnificent and I couldn't help but wonder what Mother's life had been like growing up here. As we trailed along behind the wandering hounds, Grandmother chatted about the running of such a big estate.

"I will need to take you around the estate over the next couple days and introduce you to everyone who lives in the various cottages. Let's see, you have met my Estate Manager, Malcolm Collier and of course his son, Cieran and Maude, our cook. Maude's husband, Sam, is the Head Gardener and there are three local men who work under him but they don't live on the estate and then there are the men who take care of the sheep...oh, the list just goes on and on. Payroll is a nightmare," she laughed before suddenly growing very serious

Turning to look me in the eyes, she solemnly said, "Your mother phoned this morning before you came downstairs. She was understandably very upset that you hadn't called her when you landed in Dublin, as you had promised. I can appreciate that you are upset with her, but that was beneath you Lucy."

"I did call her Grandmother but she wasn't home. The call went right to her answering machine. If you don't believe me, you can ask Mr. Collier. He was just coming back with our coffees when I ended the call."

Touching my arm, she said, "No need for that. I believe you, but why didn't you just leave a message so she wouldn't worry?"

Dropping my eyes and staring at my feet, I mumbled, "I was angry that she wasn't there waiting for me to call."

Grandmother just nodded, "I understand. Shall we go in and call her now?"

I really didn't want to because I knew I was in for another argument, but I didn't want to upset Grandmother, so I just nodded and followed her up the stairs and back into the house.

Surprisingly, the phone call didn't end in an argument. After explaining to Mother that I had called but no one answered, I held my breath waiting for her to ask why I didn't leave a message, but she didn't. I almost dropped the phone when she actually apologized saying she had forgotten to charge her cellphone. She jabbered on for a while before I was able to finally hang up and breathe a sigh of relief.

Chapter 4

Two nights passed before they finally managed to find me again. Perhaps they didn't travel with me on the plane or perhaps they'd been just sleeping off jet lag. Who knows? All I know is that they were back, and back with a vengeance, but something had radically changed. This time it wasn't just their presence I could sense, this time I could actually hear their conversations. At first, I thought it was Grandmother speaking to someone in the hallway outside my bedroom door. That was until the argument between what was obviously a man and a woman ended with the woman breaking down into muffled tears and footsteps fleeing in opposite directions down the hall.

Slipping into my robe, I crept silently to the door and hearing nothing, opened the door a crack and peered out into the hall. It was pitch dark and icy cold. No one was there only the faint smell of lavender. The long hallway was completely deserted. Feeling my way down the hall, I turned the crystal doorknob to Grandmother's bedroom and peeped inside. The moonlight filtering through the windows bathed the bed in light and I could just make out the prone, soundly sleeping figure of Grandmother.

Shaking my head to clear the sounds of the voices in the hallway from my brain, I gently pulled the door shut behind me and shuffled back to my room, climbed back into bed and pulled the duvet up to my trembling chin.

"Oh, it must have just been a dream, but I could have sworn I really did hear voices," I muttered out loud to myself as I tried to recall what was being said during the argument. All I could recall was the female voice saying, *"They could starve; they're only children for God's sake"*, before sobbing uncontrollably after the male's angry response.

Plumping up my pillow and rolling over on my side, I pulled my knees up to my chest, exhaled deeply and closed my eyes tightly before drifting off to a restless sleep. My last thought before allowing the darkness to consume me was, 'I must ask Grandmother in the morning if anyone else lives in the house and what children could be in dire need'.

The next morning, I slept later than normal and soon as I could slip into my jeans and pull my sweater over my head, I hurried down to the kitchen looking for Grandmother. Maude, Grandmother's cook, was just cleaning up from breakfast when I bounded through the door.

"Good Morning, Miss Lucy. Sit yourself down and let me get your breakfast for you."

I couldn't help but smile brightly at the elderly lady. When Mother told me I was going to live with my grandmother, this was the image of my grandmother that came to mind. I guess I really had been watching too many period dramas. Maude was rather round and wore a cap over her graying, red hair and a big white apron over her dress. Her face always had a rosy glow and she was always ready with a smile that caused her eyes to twinkle. Watching her move around the kitchen, as she scrambled some eggs for me, I wondered what her past life had been like and what brought her to Tara.

As she slid the plate in front of me and reached for the kettle, I asked, "Have you always been the cook here, Miss Maude?"

Filling my cup, Maude dropped down in the chair opposite me and said, "Oh no, Miss Lucy. I came here after my Patrick and I got married. He was already working here as under-gardener and I was working as a cooks assistant in a hotel over on the coast. We met one day when I had wandered down to the seafront on my day off. He was the most handsome man I'd ever seen and when he smiled, oh the merriment just twinkled in his eyes. I made up my mind that very day he would be my husband and six months later, he was!"

Munching on my toast, I asked, "Miss Maude, do you and your husband live here in the house?"

Pushing a strand of hair back under her cap with the back of her hand, the cook replied, "Oh no, Miss. Only your grandmother and now you live here in the big house. My husband is the head gardener now and like most of the other staff, we have cottages on the estate. Why do you ask?"

"Oh, I thought I heard voices in the hall last night."

Maude's brow furrowed as she placed the palms of her hands on the table and pushed herself up from the chair. Turning her back on me she returned to kneading the dough for the homemade breads she baked every morning before she replied over her shoulder, "Old houses like this make all sorts of strange noises, Miss Lucy."

I might only be almost sixteen but I had the sense to know when to change the subject, "Has Grandmother gone to the stables already?"

""Yes, miss. She's always down there right after breakfast. Loves her horses, she does. She rides that Dailtín of hers every morning rain or shine."

"That's a strange name for a horse. Why does she call him Dailtín? What does it mean?" I asked as I piled my scrambled eggs on to my toast, making a sandwich.

Stifling a smile, Maude said, "Dailtín is Gaelic, the language many of us Irish still speak today. It means brat and a right brat he was. Your grandmother raised him from a wee colt and he was into everything. Between kicking down fences and running wild to biting everyone who came close to him. I thought she'd never get him to the point she'd be able to ride him, but ride him she did. Mind you though, she's the only one he'll allow on his back."

Pushing my chair back causing it to loudly scrape on the slate tiles, I grabbed what was left of my sandwich and headed for the kitchen door, turning to yell over my shoulder, "Thanks for breakfast, Ms. Maude. It was delicious, as usual."

Wiping her hands on her apron, she walked to the kitchen door and held it open for me, "You're welcome Miss, if you turn right at the end of the house you'll be back on the square facing the stable."

As I reached the corner of the house, I turned, looked back and waved at a worried looking Maude, still watching me from the door. Waving goodbye before beginning to run across the cobblestones to the stable, I couldn't help thinking to myself, 'She knows more than what she's saying.'

Suddenly my feet began to slide out from under me and I found myself waving my arms around like a tight rope walker, trying to regain my balance. 'Pheww…that was close,' I thought as I straightened myself up, slowed my pace and made a mental note to walk slowly when crossing the cobblestone courtyard if it was still damp from the morning mist. I was determined to ask Grandmother what Maude might know that she wasn't telling me and why she looked so worried.

She was just returning from her morning ride when I reached the stable door. From the rosy glow on her cheeks and the sweat beading down Dailtín's flanks, it was obvious they had been riding hard. Handing the reins to a waiting Cieran, she said, "Wipe him down good. I'm afraid; we've both worked up quite a sweat."

"Yes, Ma'am," replied Cieran as he led Dailtín away, but not before looking back over his shoulder at me and winking, causing me to turn beet red again.

Seeing the look on my face, she quickly made her way out of the stable and slipped her arm around my shoulder and asked, "What is it, Lucy? You look troubled. Are you missing your parents so soon?"

"No Grandmother, it's not that but I do want to ask you something but I don't want you to think I'm crazy or something."

"I could never think that of you Lucy. It's a beautiful morning and the roses are particularly lovely this time of year. Let's sit in the garden and you can tell me what's bothering you."

Turning briefly to call to Cieran, "Please ask Maude to bring tea to the garden when you finish with Dailtín," before leading me through the gray, curved stone archway into the walled garden beyond. It was indeed a beautiful place, filled with scent of old-fashioned roses and the sound of bird song.

Leading me to a wrought iron table positioned in the perfect shaded place for enjoying the solitude of the surroundings, she reached for my hand asking," So what has upset you, child?"

Casting my eyes down at my hands, which lie clasped in my lap, I began to feel the heat rising up my neck and spreading to my cheeks. I blurted out, "I heard a man and woman arguing in the hallway outside my room last night, but when I looked they had disappeared."

Without batting an eye, she said, "Oh, is that all? I was afraid you were unhappy here."

My mouth flew open as I abruptly jumped to my feet, nearly knocking over my chair. "Is that all? Aren't you worried about strangers being in your house at night? Maude said only you and I were supposed to be in the house last night and after the argument stopped, I peeked into your room and you were asleep. So if it wasn't you, than who was it?"

Patting my now empty chair and motioning for me to sit back down, she replied, "Yes, there were just the two of us there last night."

Slowly sinking back into my chair, I gazed into her eyes and asked, "Are you saying I must have been dreaming or something?"

Our conversation was temporarily interrupted by a still frowning Maude carrying a tray laden with tea, brown bread and butter.

Once Maude had left the tray and returned to the house, Grandmother began filling the fine bone china cups with tea, passed it over to me saying, "No, you probably weren't dreaming. I'm just surprised they have made themselves known to you so soon. It appears you did inherit at least one thing from me. Tell me child, how long you have felt the presence of things that others don't."

Suddenly relieved, I stared wide-eyed into her sympathetic eyes and told her things that I had kept secret since I was a young, "I first remember feeling their presence in my bedroom but they never seem to stray past my bedroom door. I have never heard them speak before, that is, until last night."

Grandmother just sat quietly holding my hand and nodding occasionally as I rambled on about my early years and the times when I had tried to tell people about "their" presence. The tea had grown cold by the time I finished and Grandmother sat with a far-away look in her eyes. It was as if she had been transported back in time and was reliving something from her own youth. When she finally responded, it was only with six words that would forever bind us together..."It was the same with me."

Chapter 5

"Perhaps you should begin by telling me what you heard outside your room last night," said Grandmother.

Hesitating for just a moment, as I shuddered as I felt a chill run up my spine, I whispered, "A man and woman were arguing. The only thing I could make out was the woman saying something about children starving and then he shouted something I couldn't understand and she burst into tears. Then I heard footsteps going in opposite directions. They were gone when I opened the door; there was only the faint smell of lavender. After looking in the hall and finding it empty, I went to check on you,"

We sat in silence for what seemed like ages, before Grandmother began softly speaking, "Perhaps I should tell you some of the history of Tara."

I could only nod at her and stare at the massive gray stone building in front of us as she continued. "Tara is named for the Hill of Tara, a low hill in County Meath, Ireland. The hill is linked with ancient Irish chieftains called the high kings of Ireland. Tara has been in the Lacy family since its construction in the late 17th century. At that time, the estate was three times the size it is now. The first owner, Robert Lacy was a wealthy merchant and built Tara for his bride-to-be, Maeve. She was the love of his life and they lived happily here. By all accounts he was a kind and generous landowner, adored by his tenant farmers. It wasn't until Maeve had all but despaired of providing her husband with the son and heir he so desperately wanted that she fell pregnant. It was a very hard delivery and despite the best efforts of the physicians, she died. The child, a healthy son survived, leaving Robert to raise the child named John on his own. Needless to say, Robert and the entire staff spoiled the motherless child. When John finally inherited after his father's death at the ripe old age of 86, he was already middle aged and still unwed. He took for his bride a young woman half his age. It was a marriage arranged by her titled but poor father. She was named Leah and she was your great-great grandmother. I believe it was John and Leah you heard outside your room last night."

"Have you ever heard them, Grandmother?

"No, my dear, but I have always felt their presence. Like you, I always knew they were here."

"Grandmother, what did she mean by the children are starving and why was he so angry with her? Surely, if his children were in danger of staving he would have been upset too."

Holding up her hand to silence me, "The starving children weren't his. Let me explain. Did they ever teach you in school about the Irish Potato Famine?"

Shaking my head, I waited for her to continue.

"An Górta Mór, or the Great Hunger, began in 1845 when the potato crop failed in successive years. The crop failures were caused by late blight, a disease that destroyed both the leaves and the edible tubers, of the potato plant. Most of the wealth of the Lacy family came from the tenant farmers who depended on the potato crop to enable them to pay their rents and feed their families. When the blight continued, families were evicted from their homes and up to one million people died. Another million emigrated from Ireland. They were the lucky ones. There were some wealthy landowners who took pity on their tenants and tried to help them. I even read of one who actually gave money to his tenants to help them emigrate. This was very rare and John was not one of these benevolent landlords. His neglect of his tenants' suffering caused a lot of heartache for the gentle Leah."

"How horrible, but obviously great-great grandmother survived and had children or we wouldn't be having this conversation."

"Yes, she survived and she recorded all the events of that horrible time in her diaries. I have them in my room, if you would like to read them."

"Yes, I would like that very much but there's something I don't understand."

"What's that, my dear?"

"Mother told me that Ireland is famous for their salmon fishing and there must have been plenty of deer and rabbits back then, why didn't they just eat them?"

"Ahhh, well Ireland was part of the British Empire at that time and according to British law, Irish Catholics couldn't apply for fishing or hunting licenses. So they couldn't legally fish or hunt and those caught doing so were tried in court as poachers. Their pigs and cattle were sent to England to feed the British and to export for trade, while the landlords kept the fine cuts for themselves. So you see the Lacy family had plenty in their food stores while their tenants were starving."

"I see, so great-great grandmother was pleading for her husband to help his tenants."

"It sounds that way. I do know from her diaries that when John was away in Dublin on business she took food from their stores to their tenants and even risked her own health by nursing the sick and dying."

The sound of someone clearing their throat interrupted our conversation, as Maude came to collect the tea tray and call us in for lunch.

Strolling from the garden arm-in-arm, I found myself longing for evening when Grandmother said I could begin reading my great-great grandmother's diaries. It suddenly dawned on me over our lunch of cold ham and salad that the diaries might be in Gaelic, as I blurted out between mouthfuls, "Grandmother, about Leah's diaries, I can't read Gaelic."

"Oh, that's ok. Leah was educated in England and her diaries were written in English to keep their contents away from the prying eyes of some of the house servants who were undoubtedly loyal to their Master."

"I am getting the feeling that her husband was a real jerk," I ventured as my back stiffened.

Grandmother brought her linen napkin to her mouth to hide the beginnings of a smile as she said, "I do love having a young person, who's not afraid to speak her mind, in the house again. I am truly sorry for your mother's problems but I'm so very happy she sent you to me. We're going to have a wonderful time while you are here and when you must leave me, I hope you will come back often."

I didn't know how to respond to this out pouring of affection. My mother always seemed a bit on the cold side. Don't get me wrong, I had all the material things I needed, we lived in a nice house, I had nice clothes and we belonged to the best clubs but she really wasn't what anyone could call affectionate. At least not like her mother. Grandmother was certainly a lot wealthier than we would ever be but she seemed to draw her happiness from things money couldn't buy. I guess if anyone asked me to describe her in one word, it would have to be "loving."

Chapter 6

It was growing dark when Grandmother brought a cup of hot, rich cocoa and the first of Great-Great Grandmother Leah's diaries to my bedroom. Handing me the small, faded, red leather book, she placed the cocoa on my nightstand and said, "I believe this is the earliest diary. She appears to have begun writing in them just a month after coming here as a bride. I have an early start tomorrow morning, so I'll tell you goodnight now."

"Goodnight, Grandmother."

Just before she left, she leaned over and stroked my cheek with the back of her hand before placing a kiss on my forehead. It was then that I noticed her scent…it was roses.

Smiling up at her, I said, "You smell lovely. You're wearing rose perfume today."

Raising just one eyebrow, "I never wear any other scent. It's my favorite. My trademark, if you like. Your grandfather loved the scent of roses and I loved your grandfather."

"Oh well, must have been Maude's perfume I smelled."

Laughing, Grandmother said, "My dear, in all the years that Maude has been with us, I have never known her to wear either perfume or make-up."

Before I could say another word about the lavender scent I had just assumed was hers, she was gone chuckling, no doubt, at the idea of Maude in full make-up, laboring away in the kitchen over the hot stove.

Shaking my head, I took a sip of my cocoa and opened the diary to the first page and began reading.

I returned from Chapel to find that father had indeed sent the gift he had promised, when I left my childhood home to become the bride of John Lacy. I still have not forgiven him from selling me into a marriage to settle his debts, so he and my step-mother could continue to have their country house and their townhouse in Dublin. If my mother had still been alive, she would never have allowed this fate to befall me. Father had married my dear mother for love and they had been very happy. Why would he wish anything less for me? It wasn't that John was cruel to me but I did not love him the way a wife should love her husband. As for John, his interest in me revolved around me providing his heir. He was often away to Dublin on business and would bring me little trinkets and jewelry when he returned. Even when he was home he seemed to spend much of his time playing cards and drinking with his friends. But I digress; there was a card with my mysterious gift that simply read, "You will never find truer friends or fiercer protectors." I was eager to see what this gift was and asked Collins, my husband's manservant, where the package was. To my astonishment, he opened the front door and pointed to the stable block. It was raining lightly, so I slipped out of my satin house slippers and into my heavy outdoor shoes before donning my cape and heading across the cobbled courtyard to the stables beyond. The stableman, Collier, was a kindly man and truth be told, the only person on the estate to ever say a kind word to me. Entering the stable, I could hear his hearty laughter coming from a distant stall and called out to him. When he emerged from the stall, he had two of the biggest puppies I had ever seen, one tucked under each arm. As I stooped down in the fragrant smelling hay and held out my arms, he quickly laid them at my feet. As I exclaimed how big and lovely they were, he explained that they were an ancient breed, known as the Irish Wolfhound and that they would get much bigger. Now, Collier was a tall man for Irish standards, much taller than my husband, so you can imagine my shock when he held his hand high over his head and said they will be this tall when standing on their hind feet. I was smitten and since they are a boy and girl, I have decided to name them Lancelot and Guinevere.

My eyes were growing weary, as I lay the diary on the night table and switched off my bedside lamp, thinking I must ask Grandmother if her hounds are named after great-great grandmothers. I had barely slipped into a deep sleep when the guttural sounds of snarling dogs interrupted my dreams of

Leah and her hounds. I quickly bolted upright in my bed holding the duvet up to my chin. Grandmother had told me the dogs wouldn't allow a stranger in the house but someone must have gotten past them because it sounded like they were right outside my door. Surely, Grandmother couldn't be sleeping through this racket! Gathering up as much courage as I could muster, I slipped out of bed and grabbed the heavy metal poker from the fireplace as I crept silently to the door. I had just placed my hand on the cold, crystal door knob when I heard him.

"Call your beasts off! I am your husband and you have no right to bar me from our bedchamber!"

Suddenly, the scent of lavender filled the air as I heard her respond, "You will not come in this room when you have been drinking with your cronies all day. So no, I will not call off my dogs."

What followed were a course of cuss words that would have made even my father blush and the sound of footsteps retreating in the opposite direction, followed by the growling of the dogs. Just as suddenly, the scent of lavender was gone and there was nothing left for me but to go back to bed. Before I switched off my bedside lamp, I glanced at the gold-encased carriage clock; it was 3am, the witching hour.

Chapter 7

I was abruptly awakened the next morning by the violent shaking of my bed. Feeling hot breath on my face, I slowly opened one eye and then the other and found myself nose-nose with Lancelot as his amber eyes bored deeply into mine.

"What are you doing here, big fellow and why are you staring at me like that?" I cooed as I pushed myself upright by my elbows and looked around the room for his partner-in-crime, Guinevere.

My eyes alighted on Grandmother as she sat in the bedroom armchair with Guinevere sprawled out at her feet. Getting up and walking over to sit on the edge of the bed, she explained, "It's an ancient belief that wolfhounds can search the souls of people to determine their worth by looking deeply into their eyes."

Before she could finish, my head was jerked violently backward as the longest tongue I'd ever seen covered my whole face. Laughing out loud, Grandmother passed me her handkerchief before saying, "It would appear you have passed the test and if I'm not mistaken, you've just made a friend and protector for life."

Grandmother suddenly leaned forward and pulled a corded rope beside my bed. Seeing the questioning look on my face, she explained, "When you pull this cord, this rope rings a bell in what used to be the hallway of the servants quarters. Each room has one that connects to a different sized bell, with a slightly different sound; which alerts the servant assigned to the room that they are needed upstairs. I've just let Maude know we are ready for tea. So, how far did you get in the diary last night?"

"I'm afraid I was so tired I only got through the first entry and then they woke me up at 3am."

"They?"

"Yes, Grandmother, it was definitely Leah and John arguing again. John must have staggered home drunk and wanted to come into their bedroom and Leah put the dogs on him and it's her perfume I've been smelling."

Nodding, Grandmother reached over and stroked Guinevere as she said, "Lancelot and Guinevere have always protected the ladies of Tara."

"Is that why you named these two after Great-Great Grandmother's hounds?" I asked as I tried to dislodge myself from Lancelot who had decided my stomach made the perfect pillow for his big head.

"Síos," commanded Grandmother as she pointed to the floor. Lancelot loudly groaned and begrudgingly gave up his soft spot on the bed before climbing down to the floor and joining Guinevere by the chair.

Once Lancelot was off the bed, she said, "Oh, my dear it's not just that. You see, they are in fact the direct descendants of the original Lancelot and Guinevere. Throughout the generations, all of the hounds of Tara are related through either one or the other of the two first puppies given to Leah as a wedding gift."

"What an unusual wedding gift," I mused as my attention was momentarily distracted by a light tapping on my bedroom door followed by Maude's rather rotund butt backing into the room with the tray of tea.

As Grandmother poured the tea, she asked, "Do you remember the message on the card?"

"Yes, it was something about never finding truer friends or fiercer protectors."

"That's right!" she exclaimed as she dropped two sugar cubes into my milky tea and passed me the dainty, bone china cup. Lifting the cup to her lips, she frowned as she got a disapproving look in her eyes, "I think perhaps Leah's father may have heard disturbing news about his new son-in-law's reputation on his return to Dublin after the wedding and was concerned for her. Apparently, John Lacy had quite the reputation for drinking to excess and was known to have a violent temper."

Blinking rapidly to clear the mist of the past from her eyes, Grandmother quickly changed the subject, "Well, enough about the past for today.

As soon as you are dressed, join me downstairs for breakfast and then we're off for a ride. I want to show you the rest of the estate."

"But Grandmother, I told you that I don't ride." I whined.

"Fiddlesticks, my child, you're a Lacy by blood and we are all born horse women, among other things," she responded with a wink as she swept out of the room leaving me staring open-mouthed at her retreating figure, wondering what other things Grandmother was hinting at. When I refocused my attention on the chair Grandmother had vacated, I saw she had left jodhpurs and riding boots beside it. I guess, at least, I would look the part.

After a quick breakfast below stairs in the kitchen, Grandmother and I were off to the stables. We were met by Cieran just coming out of the stables, leading Grandmother's Dailtín and a beautiful while horse for me. The look of panic and sheer terror must have plainly shown on my face, because as Cieran offered his cupped hands for my foot to mount, he whispered, "Don't be afraid Miss Lucy, Bán is very gentle, we teach the wee children to ride on him."

As soon as I was mounted, Grandmother took the lead and we were off. I was surprised how easy this horseback riding was, as Bán plodded along behind Grandmother while she proudly pointed out the beauty spots of the estate. After about a butt-numbing hour, she finally turned Dailtín towards home. As soon as Tara was in sight she touched her heels to Dailtín's sides and they were off, flying across the open field, leaving me in their dust. We had only gone a little way when suddenly Bán stopped dead in his tracks and began backing up as if he could see something that I couldn't. There was nothing there except some large boulders clustered under a canopy of ancient oak trees at the side of the path. No matter how hard I tried, I couldn't get Bán to budge. The next thing I knew, I could make out someone on horseback in the distance coming towards me. Cieran was coming to the rescue.

"Is everything alright, Miss Lucy? When Mrs. Lacy came back without you and you didn't follow, I figured I should ride out and look for you. I'm glad you're ok. I was afraid you may have fallen off but it looks like old Bán has just decided he's not ready to go back to the stable yet."

Taking the reins from me, he slipped them over Bán's head, and took the lead and started back towards the stables. We had barely made it to the boulders again when Bán stopped and began pawing the ground and shaking his head up and down. Suddenly, the air grew very cold and a feeling of dread came over me. Something bad must have happened here and Bán could sense it too.

"Do you feel that?" I called to Cieran as he maneuvered Bán away from the shaded boulders and back toward the stables.

"Feel what, Miss Lucy?"

"The cold and for goodness sakes, Cieran, it's just plain Lucy! Can we just drop the Miss bit?"

"Yes ma'am. If you insist, Miss Lucy and no, I don't feel cold," replied Cieran as he looked at me strangely.

He may have tried to hide it, but I heard his chuckle of amusement as he led me back to the stable. If he thinks that's funny, he hasn't seen anything yet. I'll beat him at his little game but right now I just want to ask Grandmother if she knows what may have happened at the boulders.

Grandmother had already gone up to the house when we finally got back to the stables. Cieran quickly dismounted and reached his hands up, placed them on my waist, and lifted me to the ground as if I was light as a feather. I couldn't help but notice his well-defined muscles as he gently placed me down on the ground. Something seemed different about him this time; he was actually staring at me with the strangest look on his face.

Still mad with him for mocking me, I demanded, "What are you staring at? Have I got dirt on my face or something?"

"No, Miss Lucy, I mean Lucy. There is just something very familiar about you. Like we have met before, but that's impossible. I've never been to America and you've never been to Ireland," he softly said, his hands still laced firmly around my waist.

Reaching down and slapping his hands away from my waist, I turned quickly to walk away from him before he could see the blush rising up my face. He was the most annoying but most gorgeous boy I'd ever met.

When I entered the kitchen, Maude was leaning across the table talking excitedly with an elderly lady. From the looks of her, she appeared to be close to 90 years old. Jumping to her feet and clucking her tongue, Maude quickly pointed me in the direction of a small room off the side of the kitchen, which I later found out was called the boot room for obvious reasons. Motioning for me to sit on the long, wooden bench that stretched the full length of the small room, she stooped down and grabbed the heel of my boot and pulled off first one boot and then the other before handing me my shoes.

"Miss Lucy, I took the liberty of fetching your shoes from your room so they'd be ready when you finished your ride. The door behind you leads directly inside from the stables, so when you finish your ride, you can come in directly through there. It keeps the muck from the stable yard off my clean kitchen floors. I'll clean your boots and they'll be here when you need them tomorrow."

Apologizing for tracking muck on her clean floor, I said, "Oh, I am so sorry Maude. Really I am. Grandmother must have forgotten to tell me. Would you like me to mop up the floor? I'm quite used to mopping floors at home."

Wringing her hands on her apron, Maude shook her head and gushed, "No, Miss Lucy that would never do. When you get your shoes on, come on in the kitchen and join my mother and me for a nice cup of tea. Your grandmother is answering her correspondence so she won't miss you for a while."

"That sounds wonderful Maude and I'd love to meet your mother."

Before leaving me, Maude whispered, "I should warn you, Mother is blind as a bat and sometimes appears to be away with the fairies, if you know what I mean."

I had no idea what she meant by that but I was about to find out!

As, I entered the kitchen, always warm from the morning bread baking, Maude patted the chair beside her and began the introductions.

"Mother, may I present Miss Lucy, she's the granddaughter of Mrs. Lacy, come all the way from America to visit. Miss Lucy, my mother, Mrs. Flanagan."

I reached forward and took the extended hand of the unseeing woman as she smiled and said in a voice that could have come from a much younger woman, "Welcome to Ireland, Miss Lucy." Still holding my hand in her wrinkled hand she murmured, "Oh, but I see you have been here before, child."

A worried look came over Maude's face as she repeated, "No mother, this is Miss Lucy's first trip to Ireland."

Still clutching my hand, the old woman said, "Then it must be your dear mother who I am confusing you with. You know, I was her nanny when she was just a wee lass and such a sweet child she was. A bit on the wild side though, always disappearing for hours on that black stallion of hers. We were forever sending the hounds after her when it was time for her to come home."

"Then you know the grounds very well," I ventured.

"Yes, what is it you'd like to know?" she asked as her trembling hands released mine and felt around for her teacup.

"There are some boulders under the oak trees not far from the stable, my horse acted strange around them. Any idea why he might not have wanted to go past them?

"I have heard stories, child, but it all happened way before my life time. The old people talked of a meeting place for lovers and a violent death.

Maude abruptly slammed her teacup down and exclaimed, "Mother, don't be filling the child's head with fairy tales and talk of death. You'll be giving her the night terrors!"

I couldn't help but wonder what Maude would think of me if she knew about the unseen things that seemed to follow me around.

The old lady bowed her head as her daughter continued, "I best be getting Mother home now Miss Lucy, if you can manage on your own."

Standing to leave, I reached over and stroked the old woman's folded hands and said, "It was lovely to meet you Mrs. Flanagan. I hope we meet again soon."

The old lady just nodded and patted my hand and said, "I would like that very much. You come visit me anytime you want."

As they made their way to the back door, I turned to watch them just in time to see her Mrs. Flanagan's unseeing eyes staring at me as though she had seen a ghost from the past.

As the door closed behind them, I went in search for Grandmother. Perhaps she could tell me more about what I experienced this morning and what Mrs. Flanagan had said about the death there.

It wasn't hard to find her, Lancelot and Guinevere sat upright in front of the library door standing sentinel, guarding their Lady from any type of a surprise attack. Despite their affectionate display this morning, I still found myself calling out to Grandmother. Within seconds the library door opened and the sea of hounds parted, allowing me entrance into the library.

"Have a seat Lucy. I'm just finishing paying a few bills."

I sat quietly while she finished. When she was finished she turned to me and asked, "Well, did you enjoy your first time in the saddle today?"

Playfully rubbing my bottom, I replied, "Yes, I really did but I wanted to ask you something. Bán pulled up short and refused to go past those big boulders under the oak trees. Cieran had to come get me and even with him taking the reins, Bán still bulked at going near them."

"Really? I've never had any problems there. I wonder why."

Suddenly growing shy, I asked quietly, "Is it possible that someone may have died there?"

"Not that I ever heard. Why do you want to know?" asked Grandmother as her face took on a grave look.

"Well, aside from Bán's reaction, I felt very cold and a feeling of dread. Then there was what Maude's mother said."

"Oh, you've met Mrs. Flanagan then."

"Yes, she was having tea with Maude in the kitchen."

"She was your mother's nanny, you know. What did she say about the stones?"

"She said the village legend was the stones were a meeting place for lovers and someone had violently died there. She also said Mother used to be a bit of a wild child. I have a hard time believing that, but Maude did say her mother is often away with the fairies, whatever that means."

Laughing, Grandmother said, "Well, I wouldn't say Mrs. Flanagan was away with the fairies. That rather quaint phrase infers a person is suffering from some type of mental impairment or in Mrs. Flanagan's case, dementia. Yes, she is elderly and has gone blind, but I think that little old lady is a lot more aware of everything going on around her than she chooses to let Maude know. As for the story about the stones, I have never heard that. I wonder if there is anything in the diaries about it. I tell you what, I have two more volumes in my bedroom and I'll give them to you after dinner. Perhaps you can scan through them to see if Leah mentions the stones. But right now, how about a drive into the village? I want to get these bills in the post and besides I want to show you off to the villagers."

As I climbed into the front passenger seat of her Land Rover, Grandmother held open the back door and in piled Lancelot and Guinevere. It was a tight fit but they managed by sitting butt to butt with their massive heads hanging out each window.

"Hope you don't mind them riding along. They are so used to not having to share me with anyone that I'm afraid they'd go into a sulk if I left them at home," said Grandmother as she shifted the car into gear and headed down the long drive towards the main road.

As we drove down the tree lined drive, I asked Grandmother if Mother had really been a wild-child like Mrs. Flanagan said. Carefully maneuvering through the narrow stone entrance, built to handle horse and carriage traffic and not cars, we were on the main road before she answered.

"Yes, she certainly was a hand full. She loved to ride and spent more time in the saddle than anywhere else. That wouldn't have been a problem but there were many days when she wouldn't return until nightfall. We had to send the hounds out to find her on more than one occasion. You can imagine the embarrassment of the men searching for her when they often found her skinny dipping in the lake on moonlit nights. Her poor father was mortified."

I glanced sideways just in time to catch the smile begin to fade from Grandmother's face and I felt even more angry with my mother for her treatment of this woman who so obviously loved her despite all her faults and her abandonment of her.

It wasn't long before we reached our destination. The village was small by even Irish standards. There was only the church, a village shop, which also doubled as the post office, a pub and a gas station, which Grandmother referred to as the petrol station, surrounded on either sides by neat rows of white-washed cottages.

After a quick stop at the post office accompanied by the hounds, and a brief wander around the village, stopping to introduce me to anyone passing, Grandmother once again turned the car towards Tara.

"You have a birthday soon. Would you like to do anything special?" asked Grandmother as she barreled down the narrow lanes while I held on for dear life, praying we wouldn't come across any other cars coming the opposite way. Grandmother apparently preferred the middle of the road.

"I really don't know, let me think about it," I managed to blurt out just as the Land Rover hit a pothole and bounced causing my head to hit the roof.

Rubbing my sore head, I decided the best defense against Grandmother's driving was to simply close my eyes, hold on for dear life and pray. That is exactly what I did until we were safely back at Tara.

Chapter 8

She must have slipped quietly into my room and left the promised diaries on my pillow while I was reclined up to my neck in a warm, fragrant, bubble bath, soaking my muscles, still sore from the mornings ride, and Grandmother's jolting drive to the village. Climbing into bed as quickly as my sore muscles would allow, I plumped up the pillow, opened the first of the diaries and began scanning them for any mention of the stones or the oak grove.

"Pity, these things aren't on a computer, it sure would make my life a lot easier. One or two little clicks and it would search the whole document. The way this is going, it may take me all night," I muttered to myself.

Somewhere around 1am, I found the first mention of the mysterious stones.

The servants spy on me and report everything back to John. It's worse this week as he's away again in Dublin. You would think now that I am heavy with his child he would stay closer to home and control this insane jealousy of his. The drink makes it worse. Under its influence, he accuses me of all vile manner of things. The only peace to be found is during my walks in the forest with my beloved Lancelot and Guinevere. During our walk today, I suddenly grew very hot and sought the shelter of shade. I grew very tired and sat on the large stones in the oak grove just below the stables. That's all I recall. I must have fainted because when I came to, I was being carried in the arms of our stableman towards the house. John's man, Collins stood with his hand on his hips, staring accusingly from the door. I heard a voice close to my ears yell, "Don't just stand there, send for the doctor, man!" before darkness claimed me again. That was all I remembered until the pain woke me as I clutched the bed sheets with my hands, my labor had begun.

I skipped through the next few pages of the diary as my great-great grandmother described the birth of her son in vivid detail, something I really didn't want to know, and continued to scan for clues to the mystery of the strange stones. An hour later, I felt my eye lids begin to feel heavy and droop as I drifted into a deep sleep, still clutching the diary in my hands.

Sometime before dawn, the sounds of arguing woke me from my sleep. Yawning widely, I said out loud, "For Pete's sake, can't you two give it a rest?"

Dragging my weary body out of bed, I staggered like a drunken sailor over to the door and in my anger flung it open wide, hoping that would silence them. It didn't. The argument raged on for another ten minutes, finally ending with a threat of death to someone whose identity I had yet to discover. Things had certainly gone from bad to worse and I felt helpless knowing there was nothing I could do to change the past. There was nothing left to do but try to get back to sleep. Sleep did not come easily, as I lie staring .at the ceiling listening to the clock in the hall chiming away the hours.

When I finally managed to drag myself out of bed the next morning, it was well past nine. Stepping out of bed, I wandered over and pulled open the drapes and opened the window. It was another fine, warm day. Nothing like the depressing rain and cold Mother had so often described when I asked her about Ireland. Since I had packed clothes based on Mother's weather predictions, I was going to have to ask Grandmother to take me shopping. Pulling on a pair of jeans and the lightest shirt I'd brought, I was off on a search for Grandmother. After finding the library empty, I headed down the stone steps to the kitchen. Maude must have heard me coming and had already set a cup of tea on the table.

"I hope my mother's tall tales didn't disturb your sleep. I was worried when you didn't show up for breakfast but your grandmother said to let you sleep in," gushed Maude apologetically.

"No, I must have just been very tired from the ride yesterday. I'm not used to spending so much time outside in the fresh air."

I wasn't about to confide in Maude about the events of last night or she would be telling anyone who would listen that I was away with the fairies, like her mother.

"Would you like breakfast, Miss?"

"No, thank you, Maude, tea will do me fine. Do you know where my grandmother is this morning?"

"Yes, she is going around the gardens with my husband, preparing for Open Day."

"Open Day? What's that?"

Filing my cup with more tea, Maude said, "Once a year, your grandmother opens the house and gardens to people from outside. People come from far and wide to spend the day. It's quite fun. A lot of people come in period dress and we have a formal tea party in the gardens. Last year there were close to eighty people here for the tea alone. There's even music and dancing in the evening for those with tickets for the ball."

"That sounds like a lot of work for you," I replied as I pictured Maude slaving away to prepare tea for so many.

"Oh, I have plenty of help from all the ladies in the village. Everyone chips in to help, after all your grandmother donates everything raised to the local school. Last year, we earned enough to insure that every student had a new laptop computer," boasted Maude.

Maude had just finished speaking, when Cieran knocked at the kitchen door.

"Excuse me Maude, but Mrs. Lacy would like to speak to you about how you think the tables should be setup in the garden for the tea."

Pulling off her apron and hanging it on a hook by the door, she was gone leaving me alone with Cieran.

"Good morning Miss Lucy? Will you be wanting to ride today?"

"No thanks. It's a bit warm."

"I agree, I'm meeting some friends to go swimming later, if you'd like to come along?"

He had no sooner issued his invitation, than Grandmother came rushing into the kitchen, "That's a marvelous idea. It's going to be a hot one today and I'm sure a lot of the village boys and girls will be there. It'll give you a chance to make friends. Come along with me. I'm sure I can find a swim suit for you."

"I'll be back to get you in an hour Miss Lucy"

Soon as he was out of earshot, I pleaded with Grandmother, "Really, Grandmother, I'd rather stay here with you."

"Stuff and nonsense, I'm an old lady and you need to be with young people your own age. Besides I have urgent business to take care of today. Now, no more arguments, Cieran will be back before we know it!"

Grandmother was right as usual and I was very glad I went. The water in the lake was crystal clear and refreshing and Cieran's friends made me feel right at home. Everyone wanted to hear if America was as wonderful as they believed. I couldn't help but be reminded of something my mother often said, 'the grass always looks greener on the other side.' On the way back from the lake, we passed the stones in the grove and I shivered as I felt the chill and feeling of dread again. Cieran suddenly stopped and wrapped his towel around my shoulders, "Are you OK? You're shaking. I hope you're not getting sick."

Dropping my guard, I muttered, "No, I'm fine. It's this place. I get this strange feeling that something bad happened here."

Cieran suddenly grabbed me by my forearms and staring deeply into my eyes whispered, "My great-great grandfather's body was found here lying across those very stones. He was murdered. No one was ever convicted of his murder. He's buried in the estate cemetery. Would you like to see his grave?"

I could only nod my agreement, as Cieran took me by my hand and led me through a shady glen to a part of the estate I'd never visited. It was quiet and peaceful there and as I wandered through the grave stones, I spotted the marker for my great-great grandfather John, but unlike my other ancestors buried there, my great-great grandmother Leah was not buried at his side. Stranger still, there was no mention of her as his wife on his stone.

Cieran suddenly interrupted my thoughts, "If you are looking for your great-great grandmother Leah, you won't find her here."

Turning to face him, I asked, "Then where is she buried?"

"No one knows where she is buried or how she died. Her body was never found. The story goes that she was seen fleeing the house one winter night and never seen again. Her husband supposedly wasn't home when his man sent for help. When a search party made up of villagers she had helped during the famine gathered in the courtyard, they were met by the barking of her hounds. Someone had locked Lancelot and Guinevere in the stables. When they opened the door, they took off like the devil himself was chasing them. When the villagers finally caught up to them, it was in the gardens below the library. There was no sign of Leah but the hounds were baying mournfully and refused to be moved from the spot for three days and three nights. There was little doubt to anyone that Leah died that night in that gardens."

"How horrible, but who killed her and where did her body go?"

"The villages all suspected John, but his friends gave him an alibi and he was too powerful to go up against. As for her body, no one knows where he hid it."

We were still standing there staring at the gravestones when Lancelot and Guinevere came bounding down the path, followed closely by my grandmother.

Smiling brightly, she said," Did you enjoy your swim?"

"Yes, it was brilliant. Thanks for insisting I go."

Leaning down in front of my grandfather's grave, she cleared away the wilting flowers and replaced them with the fresh ones she had brought with her as she said, "I come here every week. Brian loved his garden and spent all his free time there planting and tending the flowers, so it's only right that he should have the fruit of his labor on his grave."

Cieran suddenly looked down at his wristwatch and boldly winked at me, "Time to see to the horses Glad you enjoyed your swim. I'll see you later Lucy."

Blushing, I couldn't help but smile as I said, "Looking forward to it."

Grandmother looked up from tending the grave just in time to catch the lingering blush and smile on my lips as I stood staring at the retreating figure of Cieran.

Quick to cut off any embarrassing questions, I quickly asked, "Do you think we could do some shopping for my birthday? Mother must have forgotten that it actually gets warm here and I don't have any suitable clothes."

Climbing to her feet, Grandmother smiled as she brushed the dirt from her hands, "Of course, we'll spend the day in Dublin. If we get an early start, we can finish shopping and I can show you all the sights."

Lacing her arm through mine, we strolled back through the woods to Tara with Grandmother chatting away about everything she thought I would find interesting in the capitol city.

Chapter 9

Two days later, Mr. Collier pulled the black Jaguar up to the front steps and Grandmother and I were off being driven to Dublin for a day of shopping. He dropped us off a block from Grafton Street where we joined the throng of shoppers, mostly tourists, wandering aimlessly down the pedestrianized street. Grandmother strode past a number of interesting small shops, then made a beeline for a rather large shop called Brown Thomas, assuring me that she was sure I could find what I needed there. Now, for a girl used to shopping at the Gap or Old Navy, browsing through the designer clothes was just a tad intimidating...not to mention the price tags. Grandmother was not to be deterred and the minute I showed any interest in anything, she scooped it up for purchase without even looking at the price tag.

When I looked over at her and complained that it was all too expensive she shrugged and replied, "As you young people would say, resistance is futile. Now, if that's everything, let's get out of here and have lunch."

I guess I shouldn't have been surprised but I was when the sales lady greeted Grandmother, "Good Morning, Mrs. Lacy. Have you found everything you need today?"

"Yes, thank you very much. Please put this on my account," she replied putting her hand on my arm before continuing, "This is my granddaughter Lucy, visiting from America. Would you be kind enough to add her name to my account in case she needs anything else while she's here and I'm unable to accompany her?"

"Yes ma'am, we'll just need you to fill out this form and we'll take care of it right away."

While Grandmother was busy filling out the paperwork, I wandered over to the door and watched the street performer who was playing a guitar and singing there. 'Didn't Ed Sheeran perform here once?' I tried to recall, scratching my head. Just have to love him. We redheads have to stick together. I was still standing there just watching the shoppers hustle back and forth when Grandmother tapped my arm, "Ready for some lunch?"

"Sure, I can always eat!" and that was the truth. Ever since I arrived in Ireland, I'd been eating like a pig, to put it mildly. I'm not sure if it was because of all the increased physical activity or that I was away from the stress at home which took away my appetite but at least I wasn't putting on the pounds, thank heavens!

Grandmother slipped her arm through mine and we strolled down the pedestrian way crowded with locals and tourists alike. Every few feet or so, I heard a distinctly American accent and remarked to her in hushed tones, "I almost feel like I'm back in America."

Grandmother just smiled as she opened the door to O'Brien's Pub, "There are two types of people in the world, my dear, those who are Irish and those who wish they were. I hope pub grub is alright for you. Don't tell Maude, but I am dying for a cheeseburger and they do a great one here. I always drop in here when I'm in town and get my fix. What about you?"

"Sounds perfect, can we get some fries too?"

"Of course but we call them chips here," replied Grandmother as she dropped our bags into a booth beside a window facing out on the street. Leaving me to people-watch, she walked up to the bar and placed our order. Within minutes, she was back balancing a pint of Guinness and a Coke.

As we waited for our lunch, Grandmother chatted away about our plans for the rest of the afternoon, "First stop is Trinity College. It's only a three minute walk from here and I think you'll really like it."

"Really Grandmother, do you think Mom plans on me being here long enough for me to worry about choosing a college?"

Our food quickly arrived and between bites of chips, Grandmother explained, "I don't know but it would be nice to have you here so close to me in my old age."

"Grandmother, you are the youngest older person I have ever met," I exclaimed as I watched her roll her eyes in delight at the first bite of her cheeseburger.

"Actually, I want you to see the Book of Kells. Surely, your mother has mentioned it."

Catching me with a mouthful, I just shook my head as she continued, "Every visitor to Ireland should see it. The Book of Kells is Ireland's greatest cultural treasure and the world's most famous medieval manuscript. The 9th century book is a richly decorated copy of the four Gospels of the life of Jesus Christ."

I really am not very religious, to say the least, and I wouldn't know one of the Gospels from another but I wasn't going to let Grandmother know. God knows what she would think of Mom and Dad if she knew I had never even stepped foot in a church in my life. Quickly changing the subject, "I hadn't heard of it but I have heard of Temple Bar. Do you think we'll have time to go there?"

"Of course, my dear, I was saving the very best for last. I was young once, too," she said winking.

Soon as we finished our burgers and chips we were off weaving in and out of the multitude of tourists heading down Grafton Street towards Trinity College. Grandmother was right about one thing, the place was mobbed. Thank goodness, the lines moved quickly, and we were soon walking over the cobbled courtyard towards the Old Library building and the exhibition. Staring at the exhibit, I soon realized she was right about another thing. I was fascinated by the beautiful manuscripts and marveled at the beauty of them and the dedication of the monks who had created them all those centuries before.

Grandmother stood silently watching the awed expression on my face before reaching for my hand and squeezing it, "Ready to go to Temple Bar now?"

"Just a few minutes more Grandmother, please," I pleaded as my eyes never left the beautifully adorned pages of the manuscript.

Ten minutes later, I found myself strolling along the River Liffey as Grandmother pointed out Ha'penny Bridge before heading south to our destination. Turning a corner, we were engulfed in a sea of tourists wandering in and out of the many bars, quirky boutiques, art galleries and souvenir shops.

"You must be thirsty by now, let's stop for a drink," shouted Grandmother over the din of the crowd. Bypassing a number of less crowded bars, she forced her way, dragging me behind her into a packed corner pub and made her way to the bar where people were standing two deep.

"It's very crowded, Grandmother. Are you sure you don't want to go somewhere else?"

"My granddaughter asked for The Temple Bar and that's what she will have," she replied as she ordered our drinks.

Looking around the bar, I soon realized what she meant. This was 'the' Temple Bar. In my ignorance, I had meant the shopping area when I asked to go here. There was no way I was going to spoil Grandmother's triumph, so in a rare show of public affection, I put my arms around her and hugged her tight in front of everyone in the bar. Shopping could wait.

Grandmother was on her second Guinness when a trio of musicians began playing on the small corner stage. They were on their second set when suddenly the man playing the fiddle looked over in our direction. As his eyes met Grandmother's, she raised her glass to him in greeting. Suddenly, the fiddling stopped as the man took to the microphone and said, "Ladies and Gentleman, we are in for a real treat today. Maureen O'Reilly is at the bar today, perhaps we can tempt her to give us a wee song."

As the applause rang out, Grandmother squeezed my hand and whispered, "Oh dear, I'm afraid there's no getting out of it. Be right back, sweetheart."

Maureen O'Reilly? I didn't even know my own grandmother's first name but from the applause in the small bar it was obvious everyone else here did. Grabbing my phone from my pocket, I googled Maureen O'Reilly. As a youthful photo of my grandmother filled the screen, I scrolled through the text and my mouth fell open. Grandmother had been a musical sensation in the 1960's before her marriage. Damn, my grandmother was a rock star!

One song quickly turned into three before Grandmother was finally able to escape her public. Eyes glowing and smiling brightly, she seemed decades younger when she rejoined me at the bar. Suddenly, cell phones appeared raised high in the air as everyone began jockeying around in the crowded bar to get a photo of her.

The bartender passed Grandmother a fresh drink and after a few sips; she winked and shouted over the noise, "Shall we go finish our shopping?"

Once we were back on the street, I grabbed Grandmother's hands and said, "You would have thought Mom would have mentioned that you were a rock star when she finally did tell me about you."

"Oh my dear, I'm afraid that's one thing you can't blame on your mother. I never discussed my career with her, as a matter of fact I must admit to being a bit secretive about my youth. I'm afraid I was a bit of a wild child. I met your grandfather one night when I was singing in that very bar and it was love at first sight. Oh, his family objected at first but he would not be swayed and we married just six months later. I came to live at Tara and Maureen O'Reilly faded into history. Now let's finish our shopping so we don't leave Mr. Collier waiting and God forbid we are late for dinner. Maude will have our hides!"

Chapter 10

It was just a week before the Open Day and I was no closer to solving the mystery surrounding my great-great grandmother Leah's disappearance and death. I had meticulously trolled through her diaries every night before bed but could find very few clues. I was shocked reading about the conditions caused by the potato crop failure and couldn't understand how my great-great grandfather could allow his tenants to starve and then put them out of their homes when they couldn't pay their rents. I marveled how Leah risked her own health to care for the sick and dying and sold her mother's jewels to pay for passage to America for her husband's evicted families. All these things she did and she was just four years older than me. I was determined more than ever to find out what happened to this good woman. With only one more diary left to read, I was beginning to give up hope.

My thoughts were interrupted by Grandmother's knock on my bedroom door and her summons to follow her. She was leading me up two more flights of stairs to a place I hadn't been before. Following her through a heavy, ancient door, I found myself in the musty, dust filled attic. There were boxes and dust covered, old trunks scattered all around the big room. Using a dust cloth she began to wipe away the years of thick layers of dust until she finally sat back on her haunches and exclaimed, "Ah ha, here it is!"

"What is it?" I asked.

Pointing to something shiny on the lock face, I leaned forward and finally saw why Grandmother was excited. The beautifully engraved initials L.L. appeared on the lid of the trunk. We had found my great-great grandmother's trunk. Carefully lifting the lid, Grandmother began folding back layers and layers of what appeared to be some type of white fabric. After a few seconds, we both gasped. Under all that material was the exact emerald green gown that great-great grandmother Leah wore for her portrait.

Lifting it gently from the trunk, Grandmother turned to face me, "I was hoping it would be here. I remember my mother mentioning it many years ago. Now, let's get this downstairs and see how it fits you."

"Me?"

"Yes, it's for you to wear to the evening festivities."

Grandmother left me to undress, while she went in search of the jewels she wanted me to wear with the gown. As I stepped into the long, flowing gown and pulled the dainty straps up over my shoulders, the scent of lavender filled the room and I heard a soft, pleading voice cry from behind me, 'Help me. You must help me.'

Slowing raising my eyes to stare into the mirror, I saw her. At first, I thought it was my own reflection until I saw the brilliant sapphires adorning her neck. I turned quickly as I heard Grandmother re-enter my room and she was gone.

"What is it, child? You're as white as a ghost!" gushed Grandmother as she rushed to my side.

"She was here, Grandmother," is all I could manage to say before sinking to the floor.

"Who, child?" she asked as she dropped down on the floor beside me.

"It was Leah. I was trying on her dress and suddenly smelled lavender and then I heard a woman's voice say, 'Help me. You must help me'. When I looked up in the mirror, she was there."

Smiling patiently, Grandmother said, "My dear, it must have just been your own reflection."

Just shaking my head as I gazed up into Grandmother's troubled eyes; I raised my hands to my bare neck and whispered, "No Grandmother, she was wearing a sapphire necklace."

Her eyes widened as she reached into the crimson, velvet bag clutched in her hand and withdrew a necklace. Hanging from her trembling fingers were the sapphires.

"They were a gift from her mother and her favorites. They were the only jewels she didn't sell during the famine. They're the ones she wore for her portrait upstairs."

We sat there on the floor in silence for a long while before Grandmother rose to her feet and reached her hand down to help me up. I could tell there was something that was deeply troubling Grandmother and I finally asked, "Is there something you know about great-great grandmother that you aren't telling me?"

"Get changed and meet me in the library. I think we both need a hot cup of sweet tea; then I'll tell you all I know about the skeletons in the closets of the Lacy family."

Grandmother was sitting slouched forward in her chair staring up at the portrait of my mother above the fireplace. She looked like she had the weight of the world resting on her narrow shoulders. I could tell by her pained expression that the news she was about to share with me wasn't going to be good.

Not even looking up at me as I entered the room, she patted the chair beside her and reached for my hand, "What I am about to tell you may come as quite a shock to you. There is no easy way of saying this, so I might as well just say it right out. There is madness in the Lacy family, my dear."

Shocked, I jumped to my feet as I asked, "Are you trying to say that I'm not really hearing and seeing things and that I'm mad?"

Quickly grabbing my hand, she said, "No, my child, not you. The madness seems only to affect the male line of the Lacy family and in most cases it skips a generation. My dear husband was perfectly sane but his father; well, he was an entirely different story."

Composing myself, I sat back down and smiled and said, "Well, that certainly is good news. Guess it was lucky you only had my mother and that I'm an only child."

Grandmother suddenly dropped my hand and turned her face away from me before she whispered, "Yes, it would have been lucky, but you see my first born child was a boy. Your mother was born six years later. By then, my once sweet, gentle son had already been placed in a facility that could care for him. That was where I had gone when you went swimming with Cieran. I always visit him every week."

"I'm so sorry, Grandmother. Mother never told me she had an older brother."

A mournful smile played across her lips as she squeezed my hand, "She didn't tell you because she doesn't know. When Michael was four, I began to notice something wasn't quite right and then one day just after his fifth birthday; I followed his laughter to the bathroom and found him. He was holding the wee puppy we had just given him under the water in the tub trying to drown him and laughing as the life began to drain from the poor thing. I arrived just in time to save the poor little creature. I was just pregnant with your mother and feared what he would do to a baby, if given the chance. Of course, we had the finest doctors examine him and the diagnosis was worse than even we imagined. For the sake of our unborn child, Michael was sent away. We hoped for years that some new treatment would be found to help him so he could return home but as the months then years passed, he became increasingly unstable, one moment appearing normal and the next extremely violent. A few months before you arrived, Michael was having one of his good days so we were sitting in the hospital's garden chatting amicably when he suddenly got up and walked behind my chair. When I turned to see what he was doing, he grabbed me by the throat and began choking me, Of course, the attendant immediately subdued him, but not before the damage was done. I wore a scarf for two weeks to hide the bruises."

I didn't know how to respond or what I could say to comfort Grandmother, so I just sat quietly holding her hand. It was Maude entering the room to bring the tea who finally broke the silence. "Is there anything else, Mrs. Lacy?"

Now composed, Grandmother smiled and said, "No, thank you Maude. This will do nicely."

After pouring our tea, I asked, "Was great-great grandfather John mad?"

"I can't say for certain, but I believe he may have become mad later in life. I know from records that he seemed quite sane when he and Leah were married. She even wrote about their loving relationship and the gifts he would bring her in the early days of their courtship and marriage. Yes, he was jealous of any male interest in her but then she was a very beautiful woman, always the center of attention at any social function. So perhaps, he was insecure. As for his quick temper, I've met very few Irishmen who didn't have a temper."

"From the arguments I've heard and the way he treated her and his tenants something must have changed."

"According to the diaries, he was spending a lot of time in Dublin and drinking heavily. The alcohol may have been the catalyst," she shrugged.

Gathering up my courage, I asked, "Grandmother, what do you think happened to Leah and where do you think she is buried?"

Putting down her teacup and taking both my hands in hers she confided, "I don't know, Lucy. I have been trying to find out for years. No one seems to know. It's like she vanished into thin air.

I think that maybe why their spirits still stay here at Tara. Perhaps they are seeking some kind of resolution."

Chapter 11

Grandmother was kept very busy the days running up to the Open Day and I found myself more in the company of Cieran. Don't get me wrong, I'm not complaining. Cieran was not only gorgeous to look at but he had a way of looking at you when you spoke. It was like he was really interested in anything you were talking about, not like the boys I knew at home who were only interested in video games or sports. Other than Grandmother, no one else really paid a bit of attention to anything I said, certainly not my mother or father. I soon found myself very comfortable in his company and began asking him about what he knew about the Lacy family.

It was another beautiful summer day. There was not a cloud in the sky, and the smell of freshly mowed grass mixed with the fragrant smell of the wildflowers in the meadow surrounding the lake filled the air. We were sitting on a blanket, enjoying a picnic lunch, packed by Maude, when I first asked him what he knew about the family history.

"My family has worked for the Lacy family for as long as anyone in the family can recall, most likely from when the manor was built. What exactly do you want to know?"

"I want to know how my great-great grandmother Leah died and where? Since, she's not in the family graveyard, then where is she buried?"

Looking away from me, Cieran stared at the sparkling blue waters of the lake as he said, "There are those who say she was murdered in the cemetery and others that she just walked into this very lake one stormy winter night."

"She killed herself and left her son to be raised by John? No, I don't think she would have ever killed herself."

"You must remember, during that time, the male heir was usually sent away at a very young age to one prestigious boarding school or another. I'm sure this was the case with her son. Leah would have just seen him only on holidays and that's even if his father sent for him."

"Well, from what I've read in Leah's diaries about John Lacy, he was so insanely jealous of everyone, I wouldn't be surprised if he wasn't even jealous of a mother's love for her child, Oh, poor Leah I'd be willing to bet she didn't get to see her son very often."

Cieran stretched out on the blanket and rolled over and lay on his back staring up at the sky. He suddenly turned his head to gaze up at me, "You look so much like her, you know. She was said to be the most beautiful woman in Ireland at the time."

Thankfully, he had turned back to stare up at the fluffy, white clouds floating by overhead, before he could see the blush spread up my cheeks. Was he trying to tell me that I looked old-fashioned or that he thought I was beautiful? Before I could gather up the courage to ask him, the unmistakable sound of snoring pierced the stillness of the lakefront. Cieran was peacefully sleeping in the warm summer sun.

All kinds of thoughts began swirling around in my head. Not only was I trying to figure out the mystery of my great-great grandmother's strange disappearance but now I was plagued with trying to figure out the workings of a fifteen year old boy's brain. Having virtually no experience with boys, I had a very strong feeling this was going to be the hardest mystery to unravel.

While Cieran napped in the warm sunshine, I slipped off my shoes, rolled up my pants legs and walked down to the water's edge. I had just waded out up to my knees and bent over to splash water in my still flushed face when I was violently shoved from behind sending me headfirst into the cold waters of the lake. Before I could struggle back on my feet, I felt the pressure of a hand on the back of my head trying to force my face back into the water. Spitting out water, I finally managed to shout, "Cieran, stop it! This isn't funny!"

In an instant, Cieran was by my side and pulling me from the water.

"What happened, Lucy? Did you slip and fall in?"

Shoving him away, I yelled, "You know very well what happened. You could have drowned me, you idiot!"

Grabbing me by both arms, Cieran pulled me around to face him and looked deeply into my eyes, "Lucy, I don't know what you think I did, but I haven't left that blanket until I heard you call my name just now."

"Well, someone pushed me in and then tried to hold my head underwater," I stammered.

As he grabbed the blanket from the ground and wrapped it around my trembling shoulders he reassured me, "It wasn't me Lucy. I would never do anything to hurt you. Never!"

I was suddenly very cold as the realization of what had just happened enveloped me. If it wasn't Cieran and no one else was anywhere in sight then it must have been the spirit of my great-great grandfather. Perhaps, this is what happened to great-great grandmother Leah. Could she have met her death in this very lake and if so why hadn't her body ever surfaced?

Chapter 12

The ball was ready to begin when I saw the shadowy figure, holding a candlestick high in the air, moving slowly down the grand staircase. I looked around for Cieran but he was nowhere in sight and afraid I would lose sight of the apparition, I followed on my own. The ghostly figure stopped momentarily in front of the library door before appearing to vanish. Slowly approaching the door, I reached for the door knob. It was ice cold like the air around the massive door. I pushed the door open and silently crept in. A feeling of dread came over me as I saw the figure standing in front of the fireplace. The room was bathed in the soft light of candles causing long shadows to move across the old-fashioned wallpapered walls. It was like the room had been caught in some type of time warp and transported back through the centuries.

Suddenly, the scent of lavender filled the room as I heard her voice, "Dearest John, won't you come back to the ball? All our guests are asking for you."

She stood head bowed with clasped hands waiting patiently for his reply until the silence was broken by the sound of glass breaking, as he threw the crystal goblet he had been drinking from into the fireplace.

"Why should I? They don't come here to see me. It is you who they come to see, the most beautiful woman in Ireland. Isn't that what they call you? I am warning you, my dear wife, that I will not tolerate your behavior anymore. Did you think I didn't know about you and every other man, even the hired help? Well, you're wrong. I know everything and I intend to put an end to it one way or another."

"John, you have had too much to drink. There is nothing going on. You know that I have always been faithful to you."

"You're a liar!"

Suddenly, the mist in the library cleared and for the first time I could clearly see John as he quickly approached Lucy and smacked her violently, first on one cheek and then the other, causing her to cry out in pain as her head jerked backward. r.

Her scream must have alerted someone in the hall, because suddenly the door swung open and a tall, dark haired man entered, shouting, "What's going on in here?"

By now John had released the grip on Leah's arms and she had sunk to the floor covering her face and weeping.

"Well, if it isn't Collier. I might have known. Have you come to your lover's rescue?"

"You're drunk Master Lacy and talking nonsense. Why don't you let me help you to your room and I'll call Mistress Leah's maid to attend to her."

As he stormed out of the library, John turned and sneered, "You will pay for this. Both of you will pay!"

Leaning over the stricken woman, Collier gently asked, "Are you alright, Mrs. Lacy. Can I do anything to help?"

Looking up at the estate manager with tears streaming down her cheeks, she reached up and touched his sleeve, "Thank you, Mr. Collier, but no one can do anything to help and I'm afraid you may have put yourself in danger now."

I shrank back against the wall fearing John had returned and planned on murdering one or both of them in front of me as I heard the library doorknob begin to turn again, To my relief, it was Cieran.

When I turned my attention back to the scene that had been playing out in front of me, they were gone and the room transformed back to its present-day state.

"There you are! Your Grandmother is looking for you," called Cieran from the doorway.

Seeing my ashen face, he was quickly by my side, taking my hand, "You're hand is cold as ice. Are you alright?"

"Yes, I mean no," I stuttered.

Laughing he asked, "Well, which is it?"

"I'm ok, Cieran but I think I may know who killed your great-great grandfather and why."

Putting his arms around my shoulder and leaning dangerously close to my lips, I felt my heart flip over before he half laughed, as he asked, "You haven't been drinking the punch have you? It's spiked, you know."

Realizing he had been just smelling my breath and wasn't planning on giving me my first kiss, I turned beet red, I stammered, "No, I haven't!"

"Then what's wrong with you and what are you talking about?"

I decided the time had come to tell Cieran about what my grandmother referred to as my "gift." As I explained the strange feelings I had experienced growing up in America and how they had suddenly grown much stronger since coming to Ireland he began to nod, as if he understood.

As he opened his mouth to respond, I blurted out, "I suppose you think I'm mad like the rest of the Lacy's."

Taking my hand gently in his, he gazed deeply into my frightened eyes and said, "That, I don't. You see, my grandmother had the "gift" too. She could hear and see things from the past and even into the future. People came from miles around to seek her help."

Our sharing of secrets was abruptly interrupted by the door flying open causing Cieran to drop my hand and push me behind him, taking up a protective stance.

"There you two are! Everyone is asking to meet my beautiful granddaughter from America," Grandmother gushed as she came forward and grabbed me by the hand and virtually dragged me from the library.

"But Grandmother, I need to tell you something really important," I blurted out.

Stopping in the hall outside the ballroom, Grandmother pulled up short and took me by my shoulders and sternly said, "Duty first, my dear and our duty is to entertain our guests. We can talk later. This mystery of ours has remained unsolved for generations; surely another few hours won't matter. Besides, I have a surprise for you!"

Pushing the massive double-doors to the ballroom open, Grandmother laced her arm through mine and led me into the crowded ballroom and face-to-face with my mother. I was too stunned at seeing her that I was left speechless.

Reaching down and taking both my hands in hers, she stepped back and smiled at me, "Lucy, you look absolutely beautiful."

This was the first time I ever recalled my mother ever giving me a complement, let alone told me that I looked beautiful and I couldn't make up my mind if I was pleased or angry at being ignored for the first sixteen years of my life.

My anger and temper won out as I lashed out, "Mother, what are you doing here?"

The smile on her face quickly faded and tears welled up in her eyes, but I was so angry that I didn't notice. It wasn't until later when Cieran took me aside, "I have never seen that side of you before, Miss Lucy."

"Oh, so I'm back to being Miss Lucy all of a sudden?"

"Yes, if you're going to act like the spoiled heiress and speak to someone like that, especially your own mother, then I'm not so sure that we should be on a first name basis," he replied as he turned to walk away,

I quickly reached out and grabbed his arm, "Please wait, Cieran. Let me explain. Can we talk in the garden?"

Just nodding, Cieran laced my arm through his and led me through the double doors and down the curving staircase to the garden and to the bench below. The night was warm and the smell of peat fires from cottages on the estate filled the moonlit garden. It was a perfect romantic setting but from the look of disapproval on Cieran's face, it wasn't romance that was on his mind. .

"Really Lucy, I can't believe you were so rude to your own mother. The poor woman left the room in tears."

Jumping to my feet, I exclaimed, "Really, well I didn't see that and you know nothing about my relationship with my mother, so you really have no right to judge me. You just don't understand!"

"Then make me understand, Lucy!" came his angry response as his eyes flashed.

"My mother has never had the time of day for me. It has never mattered to her what I have wanted or needed. She didn't even tell me that I had a living grandmother until she found it convenient for her. If you think I'm cruel, then you're going to think she is a real monster. Do you know, this is the first time she has spoken to her mother, let alone been home since she left seventeen years ago? She deprived me of knowing my grandmother and now she is depriving me of my father."

Slowly getting to his feet, Cieran wrapped his arms around me as my emotions got the best of me and I burst into tears.

"So, this is really what it's all about. It's your mother and father divorcing," he gently said as he patted my back.

I don't think I realized it at the time but it suddenly hit me that Cieran was right. It wasn't so much the fact that they were divorcing but that they didn't think I should be even considered in the process.

By sending me away so they could fight over material things, I felt like I meant no more to them than one of their leased cars, something to be sent away when they didn't have a use for it anymore.

As soon as I composed myself, Cieran suggested, "I'm not trying to tell you what to do, but your mother has come all this way and since she hasn't come to see her mother in all these years, she must have come to see you. The way I see it, she must value you very much. Why don't you talk to her, just see what she has to say."

All I could do was nod, as he took my arm and lead me through the garden and back up the marble steps to the ballroom where my mother and Grandmother were waiting. Grandmother was quickly by my side and smiling her usual relaxed smile as she reminded me of the duties of the family as hosts, "You can speak with your mother after the guests leave but for now, we'll have no more of that behavior. It is unbecoming behavior for the future owner of Tara."

My mouth flew open to ask her what in the world she was talking about but she was away to mingle with her guests leaving me staring wide-eyed after her elegant, retreating figure.

Chapter 13

The ball went on until midnight and it was another hour before all of the guests had passed through the ancient front door on their way home. I was exhausted after dancing with what seemed like every man there from ten to eighty but not with the one person who I really wanted to dance with. Cieran had mysteriously disappeared half way through the evening without even saying goodbye. Grandmother and Mother headed for the library for a glass of wine before bed and were deep in conversation when I looked into the room.

"I'm not interrupting am I?" I called from the doorway, determined to strike a conciliatory note with my mother as Cieran suggested.

Grandmother called, "Not at all, dear. Come join us. Would you like a glass of wine?"

Before I could even refuse, all hopes of a reconciliation ended as Mother abruptly cut me off. "For goodness sakes Mother, she's only fourteen. Don't you think that's a bit young for wine?"

Irritated at the way she snapped at the grandmother who had been nothing but loving to me, I snapped, "Actually Mother, I'm sixteen and you would know that if you ever spent even five minutes of your precious time thinking about me and not yourself for once in your life!"

Reaching over and slipping a calming hand over my clenched fists, Grandmother said, "I think it's been a very long day and everyone is over-tired. Perhaps it's time for us to retire for the evening."

Seeing the pleading look in her eyes, I leaned forward and kissed her cheek and left the room without looking back. After I left the room, I stood listening at the door long enough to hear my mother say, "Well, that didn't go very well."

"What did you expect, Patricia? Don't you ever learn? When will you learn what is really important in your life? Now, if you excuse me, I'm off to give Lancelot and Genevieve their evening walk. If you want to sleep in your bed tonight, I would suggest you go upstairs before I return. You may be my daughter but you are a stranger to them and once I go upstairs, they won't let anyone pass."

Quickly running up the stairs, I was out of sight before Grandmother and her hounds left the library for their walk.

It seemed very cold in my bedroom when I walked in, but I was too wired up from the events of the evening to curl up under my warm duvet and fall asleep so I pulled up a chair and reached for another one of great-great grandmother's diaries.

John could be so kind when it suited him and when he wasn't drinking, but those days are getting fewer and father between and his behavior has grown completely irrational. My dear son has not been home for the last six months, not even for Christmas. I hate to believe that John's jealousy extends even to his own son and heir. Yesterday, he sent away my ladies maid, the one and only connection to my happy and carefree life before marrying and moving here. This house has become like a prison to me. All that I have left is my Lancelot and Guinevere and I worry for them.

Suddenly, I felt my great-great grandmother's necklace tighten around my neck. Whirling about I could see him standing in the mist behind me, smiling his sardonic smile. He was choking me. My hand went to my throat as I tried to slip my fingers between the necklace and the soft, vulnerable skin of my throat. The air was being choked out of me and I opened my mouth but nothing would come out. I couldn't even call out for help. Just as I was about to lose consciousness I heard them, as their guttural snarls filled the room. They had somehow managed to get into my room through the closed door. Thank god, Lancelot and Guinevere frightened off my attacker but not before I heard his oath as I drifted into unconsciousness, "Filthy beasts, you'll pay for this!"

When I came to, I was alone, the necklace lay on the floor behind me and the door was closed. Grabbing the necklace and creeping to the door, I opened it and peered out into the hall. There was no sign of Lancelot or Guinevere as I tiptoed down the hall to Grandmother's room. Maybe, I had just been over tired or imagined it but I still wanted to return the necklace to Grandmother.

When I entered the room, Grandmother was still awake and sitting in front of the dressing table mirror, putting cold cream on her face. When I walked up behind her, her eyes grew wide and she gasped, "My child, what happened to your neck?"

Looking in the mirror, my hand went involuntarily to my throat when I saw at once what Grandmother was talking about. It hadn't been a dream after all, and it wasn't my imagination. I had been strangled. The swollen, red welt around my neck was undeniable evidence of it.

I quickly told Grandmother what happened in my room and told her how her hounds had saved me. When I had finished talking, Grandmother turned and stared towards the far corner of the room where Lancelot and Guinevere lay curled up, watching us, "Lucy, it couldn't have been my hounds. They haven't left that spot since I came upstairs."

"Good grief, not only am I seeing John and Leah but now her hounds are making themselves known. I still haven't told you about what I saw in the library before the ball."

Going over to her bed, Grandmother patted it and said, "That can wait until the morning. You best stay in here with me tonight. You'll be safe in here. I brought the hounds up tonight in case your mother wanted to go downstairs early. With the difference in time zones between here and the States, she'll likely wakeup and still be on East Coast time."

"Speaking of Mother," I began screwing my mouth up in a frown.

Grandmother was quick to interrupt me as she tucked me into her bed and climbed in beside me, "No, that's another subject that can wait until the morning. Things always look better in the morning."

Placing a kiss on my forehead, she switched off the bedside lamp and was soon softly snoring. Sleep came slower for me as the events of the evening played over and over in my mind. The only thing visible in the darken bedroom was the red glow from the eyes of Lancelot and Guinevere as they kept watch through the dark of night. As I drifted off to sleep, I worried about the threat John had made against the hounds and worried that if his spirit could physically hurt me then he would do something to harm Grandmother's hounds.

Chapter 14

I passed the night peacefully, knowing the hounds were on guard, and woke before Grandmother. Wandering over to her dressing table, I saw the evidence of last night's attack reflected in the mirror and decided to cover it with one of the many scarves Grandmother had hanging in her closet.

Slipping quickly into Grandmother's ensuite bathroom, I quickly showered and wrapped myself in one of the thick white robes that hung from the ornate hook on the back of door before tiptoeing out of the room and heading to my bedroom to get dressed.

My return to Grandmother's bedroom roused Lancelot and Guinevere from their beds and their warning growl was enough to wake Grandmother who looked up and smiled in my direction then rolled over on her back and stretched her arms over her head.

"Good Morning, Lucy. Did you sleep well?"

"Yes, when I finally fell asleep. My brain was racing and I didn't seem to be able to turn it off." I replied as I tied the chosen scarf loosely around my neck.

"Ugh, I hate when that happens! That was some party last night, wasn't it? And you, my darling child, were the belle of the ball. Let me get a quick shower and I'll be right back," she replied as she climbed out of bed and silently padded to the bathroom.

I spent the next 20 minutes while I waited for Grandmother sitting on the floor playing with Lancelot and Guinevere as they gently investigated the scarf around my neck, as if trying to uncover what secrets it held. As soon as Grandmother emerged and was ready to go downstairs, I was abandoned as they took their positions on either side of their mistress.

Grandmother predicted right, Mother was already finished her coffee and was staring out the library window at the gardens below by the time we showered, dressed and made our way downstairs.

Turning as she heard us enter the room, she smiled brightly and said, "I never grow tired of this view. I had forgotten how much I missed it."

Reading the anger in my eyes, Grandmother quickly interrupted me before I had the chance to blurt out that it was just like Mother to comment on missing a view rather than the woman who had given birth to her, "Coffee or tea, Lucy?"

Mother never allowed me to drink coffee at home, so just to piss her off, I responded 'coffee', and waited for her to object. Unlike last night, she remained silent and expressionless.

Pouring the coffee, Grandmother motioned for us both to sit before looking from one of us to the other before resting her gaze on my mother.

"Patricia, your daughter is old enough to be told what is going on between you and her father and what your plans are for the future. and Lucy your mother must be told about what has been happening since your arrival here. Now, who wants to go first?"

Not waiting, I jumped to my feet and yanked the scarf away from my neck. Mother's response was far from what I expected, as her eyes widened and filled with tears, "Oh Lucy, I'm so sorry. I had no idea my separating from your father would cause you to try to harm yourself."

"Oh for God's sake Mother, I didn't do this to myself and everything isn't always about you!"

Grandmother could see things weren't going the way she hoped and quickly interrupted, "Lucy, I would like to speak with your mother alone. Would you be kind enough to take Lancelot and Guinevere for their morning walk?"

I was only too glad to have an excuse to get away from my mother's company and stormed out of the room. Closing the library door behind me, I walked to the front door with Grandmother's loyal hounds plodding along behind me. Once across the courtyard, they were off to the meadow racing around after each other, only stopping occasionally for what Grandmother called some 'face fighting.' I was accustomed to this method of play now but the first time I witnessed the two hounds going at each other with lips curled and massive fangs bared, it had sent me screaming for Grandmother to intercede. Watching them like this, in their natural surroundings, it was easy to understand why the Lacy family had always kept and bred this magnificent breed.

Once finished their play, they slowly ambled back towards the house, stopping only once for a long drink from the fountain before heading back through the open front door. Once inside, I found the library door open. Grandmother was nowhere to be seen, only Mother sitting alone on the sofa.

"Where's Grandmother?" I snapped diverting my eyes so I wouldn't have to look at her.

"She's gone to the stables. Please sit down Lucy. Your grandmother has told me everything," she asked as I dropped into the nearest chair.

"Everything?"

"Yes, everything. She told me about my brother and the mental illness in the family."

Clenching my fists, I retorted, "So, you think I'm mentally ill, as you politely put it? How very politically correct you are, Mother!"

Grabbing my arm before I could leap from my chair, she whispered, "No Lucy, I do not. The fact is, while only some male members of the Lacy family have this illness, all female members of the family have the gift of sensing or hearing things that others cannot."

Slowly, dropping back into my chair, I gazed into my mother's sympathetic eyes and asked, "You too, Mother?"

"Yes darling, me too, growing up here I could sense there was a presence in the house. I could smell the scent of lavender and feel cold spots even during the hottest days of summer. Unlike you, I never heard them or saw them, let alone was attracted by them. I am so sorry I always pretended that what you were sensing did not exist. I just was trying to protect you from the ridicule I faced when I was young. People can be very cruel."

My shoulders drooped in relief as I sighed and leaned against her, "Then, you do believe me?"

Wrapping both her arms around me and pulling me close, Mother said, "Yes, I do believe you and I have phoned your dad. He'll be on the next flight over and between all of us; we'll solve the mystery and put these spirits to rest."

"Dad is coming here?"

"Yes, your father and I had been working very hard to try to save our marriage but I was having problems forgetting the past. He has been doing really well with trying to change things in his behavior that weren't, shall we say, working. I'll admit that breaking my bad habits, as you witnessed last night, is a work in progress, but that's what brings me to why I'm here. I soon came to realize that most of what was wrong with our marriage was my fault. Then I panicked and realized how much I missed that one person in my life who I loved more than life itself. I missed you and, without sounding like a complete baby, I wanted my mother."

Casting my eyes down, I mumbled, "I've always blamed myself, you know. I felt like all the arguments were my fault."

Suddenly wiping away the tears that streamed down her cheeks and bursting into laughter, she grabbed me into her arms again and said, "Goodness no; your father and I have been fighting since the first day we met. As a matter of fact, that's how we met, arguing over something so stupid I don't even remember what it was"

Watching my mother's eyes light-up as she talked about my father, I realized despite their constant bickering she must still be in love with him and asked, "Mother, how did you and Dad meet? You have never told me."

Taking me by my shoulders, she gently turned me to face the portrait of her that hung over the fireplace, "Your father was an artist before becoming an architect and it was him who painted my portrait. Now, let's go find your grandmother. I'm sure she's worried about us."

Turning back at the door to gaze at her portrait, I thought, 'Well, that explains why my mother looked so happy in her portrait. She was in love.'

Closing the door behind me, I muttered, "Well, that solves one mystery."

"Mystery?" asked Mother.

"Oh, nothing Mother. I was just thinking about something Grandmother told me."

Grandmother was just crossing the courtyard with Cieran heading for the library by the time we made our way down the front steps, "Time to get busy solving this mystery. I don't know about you but I'm quite tired of having uninvited guests in my house."

After ringing for Maude to bring tea, Grandmother paced up and down in front of the fireplace laying out her plan of action.

Once Maude had left the tea and disappeared back to the kitchen, I announced, "In all the excitement, I haven't had the chance to tell anyone about what happened in the library the night of the ball."

As I started to recant what I had witnessed in the library that night, Cieran sat as still as a statue and just as quiet, his gaze locked on my neck, before he jumped to his feet and demanded, "What's happened to your neck?"

Before I could explain, Grandmother interrupted, "It appears that Lucy's likeness to her great-great grandmother has put her directly in the firing line of John's wrath."

Cieran's face grew grave as the veins on his neck began to stick out as he clenched his fist and stared into my eyes, "It was him down at the lake, wasn't it?"

Grandmother and Mother exchanged worried looks before Grandmother asked, "Lucy, what happened at the lake?"

"Cieran and I had gone down to the lake and were having a picnic, Cieran dozed off and I was warm so I was just wadding around the shore when someone grabbed me from behind and pushed my head under water. Honestly, I thought it was Cieran just messing around but it wasn't. I screamed and he woke up and pulled me out of the water. There was no one else in sight."

"You should have told me, child. It's not safe for you to be left alone now."

Mother reached over and took my hand as she stared into Cieran's troubled eyes, "That brings us to why you're here, Cieran. If the ghost of John can physically attack Lucy because of her resemblance to his wife, there is a possibility he may go after you."

"Why me?" asked Cieran.

"Because your great-great grandfather was the only ally Leah had here at Tara, after her ladies maid was sent away."

"Yes, but that was my great-great grandfather and not me."

Mother suddenly stood and walked over to a large gold framed painting at the far end of the library. Standing in front of the century-old, oil painting of a massive black stallion posed proudly in front of Tara she said, "The gentleman holding the reins of John's prize winning stallion in this painting is your great-great grandfather Collier. I don't think there can be any question that you look a lot like him."

Holding my hand up to interrupt my mother, I gazed into Cieran's confused eyes, "Before the ball I saw an argument between Leah and John, in this very room. John was drunk and accusing Leah of being unfaithful. When she denied it, he slapped her. Your great-great grandfather must have been in the hallway, heard the noise and came to her aid. John threatened both of them. Leah was worried that your great-great grandfather had put himself in grave danger."

"Alright, we have a starting point. I can check the household records and find when the ball occurred. Now Cieran, your family has always said your great-great grandfather was mysteriously murdered, and the crime went unsolved. Can you ask around and see if you can find out anything else?" asked Grandmother.

"I will, but don't worry about me. I can take care of myself. Just take care that Lucy isn't harmed again."

"Don't worry Cieran. We won't let her out of our sight. You just be careful. Don't take any unnecessary risks. Try not to be alone."

With that, Cieran was up and out the door, leaving all eyes turned towards me as a deep, pink blush spread up my neck to my cheeks. Sensing my embarrassment, Grandmother quickly looked away but not Mother. It was as if she had seen me in an entirely new light. While she sat there with her mouth slightly open and her eyes wide, I quickly made my escape from the room, nearly falling over Grandmother's hounds in the process.

As I quietly pulled the door shut behind me, I heard Mother say, "I think my little girl is growing up."

"Yes, and that is why I have named her heir to Tara. She has blossomed here and I believe she loves it as much as I do, and in a way that I don't think you ever could. I hope you aren't disappointed at being passed over, Patricia."

"Of course not Mother, but you have many years ahead of you as mistress of Tara and who knows in what direction our Lucy's life will take her."

"True, but then no one could have conceived all those years ago, that I would give up a promising career, a chance to see the world and fame and fortune to marry your father and settle down here in the country."

Mother and daughter remained sitting comfortably chatting as if it was only yesterday and not the seventeen years since their estrangement. Reaching over and taking her mother's hand in hers, Patricia gazed into her mother's eyes and calling her by the name she hadn't used since childhood asked, "Mommy, did you ever have any regrets?"

"What do you mean by regrets?"

Reaching over on the side table and picking up a silver framed photograph of a man standing in the garden proudly pointing at a beautifully blooming rose bush, her eyes teared up, "Did you ever regret giving everything up to marry Daddy?"

Reaching over and clutching her daughter's free hand, she replied with a sigh, "No, my dear. My life with your father had its ups and downs, like any married couple, but I never regretted one minute of it. My only regret was that he left us way too soon. I still miss him every single day."

Sniffling loudly now, Patricia asked, "Haven't you been lonely? Have you never thought of marrying again in all these years? I'm sure you've had many opportunities."

"A few, but none who could hold a candle to your father, beside I haven't been alone here and I knew one day you'd return. Now enough about the past, I believe my son-in-law shall be arriving soon. Perhaps now, since Lucy isn't here, is a good time for you to tell me of your plans."

"For years, Michael has been locked into a profession that he hated. I was so wrapped up in my own career that I didn't even notice the warning signs. I neglected my husband and Lucy for pursuit of the almighty dollar. I forgot about the important things in life to chase after my perception of the American dream."

"I'm sorry, Patricia, I'm not following you."

"Quite simply put Mother, Michael hated being an architect. Yes, he had reached the top of his profession but he hated it. He dreaded even going to work in the morning and I didn't even notice. He was just trying to make lots of money so I could live the lifestyle that I felt I was entitled to. Basically, that's the problem in a word...entitlement. Mother, I am a spoiled brat and I've messed up everything!" continued Patricia before covering her face with her hands and bursting into tears.

Taking a deep breath before leaning over to wrap her arms around her daughter, Maureen asked, "Now that you recognize the problem, what do you intend to do about it?"

"Well, Michael and I have done a lot of talking and Michael really wants to return to painting. We have enough money saved so it wouldn't be a problem. We wanted to speak with you and ask how you would feel about us selling our house and moving back here to be close to you. That's if you are even willing to forgive us for the way we've ignored you all these years. And then there's Lucy, we don't want to do anything that might make Lucy more upset and unhappy than our silly arguments have over the last few years."

"That of course is something you'll have to discuss with Lucy. Would you be staying here at Tara?"

Patricia rose to her feet and walking to the window that looked over the gardens, sighed loudly before continuing, "We would love to live here as long as it is alright with you and that's only if Lucy won't be upset about not returning to the States."

Joining her daughter at the window, Maureen slipped her arm around her daughter's shoulder and pointed towards the old stone barn that had lain vacant for years since cattle were no longer kept on the estate, "You know that old barn could be converted into a beautiful home and hay loft would make a fantastic artist's studio. What do you think?"

Eyes brimming with tears, Patricia turned to her mother, "It would be perfect, Mother. You always know the right things to say and do."

Shaking her head as she grasped her daughter's hands in hers and stared into her eyes, "Not always my dear child or I wouldn't have argued with you seventeen years ago and lost precious time with you."

The shrill of the hall telephone ringing startled the sleeping hounds as they commenced howling, interrupting the tender reunion between mother and daughter.

Shooing the circling hounds out the open front door, Maureen grabbed the phone, "Hello. Yes, hello Michael. I am fine and you? Yes, hold on one moment and I'll get Patricia for you. Yes, it has been way too long and I'm looking forward to your arrival."

Handing the phone to her daughter, Maureen walked out into the sunshine in search of her granddaughter.

Chapter 15

It was another week before Dad could arrange for a realtor to handle the sale of our home in America and contract the moving company to arrange for transport of our household goods to Ireland. I could tell that Mother and Grandmother were excited about being a family again after so many years and I was beginning to get used to the idea that Ireland would be my home for some years to come.

Things had been very quiet in the house lately. It was as if the spirits of John and Leah knew there were big changes coming to Tara. Perhaps with the arrival of my father, John would be less eager to show himself. From everything I had learned about John Lacy, he seemed to be a coward when it came to physically confronting other men but had no problem being abusive to his wife and any other woman that challenged his authority.

And so it was. With the arrival of Father, the only sign that there was any paranormal activity at Tara was the faint smell of lavender that I would often sense, especially lately around Guinevere and Lancelot. One morning, as I came down for breakfast, I smelled a strong scent of lavender and witnessed both hounds happily rolling over on their backs and moaning contently, as if they were getting their favorite belly rubs.

Over breakfast, I mentioned what I had witnessed and Grandmother suddenly stopped eating, "I thought that it was your father's presence that had kept John away, but I don't think that is it now."

Mother looked disappointed at the idea that the visitations might return because she was hoping to be able to move out of my room and in with my father "If it's not because of Michael who do you think it is?

"Do you recall that the diaries always mentioned how worried Leah got when John would be away in Dublin? I have a feeling that he may have chosen this particular time for one such trip. That would explain Leah's sudden attachment to the hounds."

"That's right, Grandmother. I remember how she feared that he would come home drunk and abusive. Since her maid had been sent away and the staff reported her every move to their master, she only had her hounds for comfort. So it makes sense."

Snorting loudly, Mother pushed away from the table and tea cup in hand walked to the window where she could observe Dad directing the work on the old barn that was to become their home. Despite it being Christmas week, the weather had remained dry enough to allow the workers to make good progress.

116

Dragging herself away from the window, Mother agreed, "Well, I guess we just better hope that he stays away for a long, long time."

After breakfast, Grandmother asked Cieran to join us and we were all soon in the attic, up to our elbows in dust, hunting through boxes of household records hoping to pin down the date of the ball. We had been going at it an hour, heaving boxes here and there, when Grandmother shouted, "I think I have it! Cieran, what was the date of your great-great grandfather's death?"

"I'm not sure. To tell you the truth, His gravestone is really old and his dates have faded from the elements and what remains is covered with ivy, so I never really could read the date. "

"We will need to have you check that. There is an old trick to reading dates on old stones. It's similar to doing brass rubbings. When you go down to the graveyard, take some paper and charcoal, lay the paper against the dates and rub it with the charcoal. It may or may not work but it's worth a try. The records mention that there was a ball held here on December 23rd. Lucy, do you remember anything else about the argument between Leah and John?"

"Like what, Grandmother?"

"What did the room look like? Was there a fire in the fireplace? Any decorations you noticed?"

I closed my eyes tight and tried to visualize the room again in my mind, "There was a roaring fire. I remember that because when John threw his drink into it, it flared up and I was afraid the greens on the mantle would catch fire."

"Like the greens we have on the mantle now? Christmas greens, Lucy?" asked Mother.

Just nodding, I turned to Grandmother, "Even if Cieran's great-great grandfather was murdered sometime after the argument at the ball it still doesn't prove great-great grandfather John did it."

Grandmother returned the large household ledger to its box and agreed, "I'm afraid that's true and unless we can unearth some other clues, I'm afraid we'll never find out what happened to Leah and Mr. Collier."

The sudden smell of lavender, wafting through the musty attic had me on my feet in a second. I'm sure I looked like one of those bloodhound dogs as I followed my nose to a stack of dust covered trunks pushed deep under the eaves of the attic. As I approached the corner the scent got stronger and stronger until I grabbed the dust cloth and began wiping off the brass label. Suddenly, the scent was gone as quickly as it had arrived and I found myself stating down at the initials J.J.L.

"Grandmother, come quick. I think I've found great-great-grandfather John's chest. Maybe there's a clue inside."

Staring down at the chest, she asked, "What brought you to this chest?"

Feeling slightly embarrassed that I had in all likelihood been sniffing the air like a dog, I stared into her worried eyes, "I smelled Leah's lavender and I kept following it until it led me here."

Gently rubbing her hand across the initials on the brass plate, Grandmother smiled, "I thought as much. This isn't your great-great-grandfather John's chest. His middle initial was C. This chest belongs to Leah's beloved son, John Joseph Lacy. She must have a reason for leading you to it so I think we'd better open it."

After carefully removing the old linens, we found a stack of small journals. They were all blue and monogrammed in gold with J.J.L. As grandmother gently removed the old journals and laid them aside she suddenly stopped and sat back on her haunches and began unwrapping something that was carefully packed in layers of expensive silk cloth.

"What is it, Grandmother?"

"There's another journal here but this one looks older and it's red like Leah's."

"I thought we had them all!"

Opening the diary, Grandmother shook her head, "from the way he has wrapped it, Leah's son must have felt that this diary was very important."

"Perhaps it holds the clues to what happened to Leah," volunteered Mother.

Grandmother handed each of us a stack of diaries as we left the musty attic and made our way downstairs to the library, "I think we'll need to read all of these if we're to find out why her son saved just this one in his personal trunk."

"I agree, Grandmother. We don't really know for certain what happened to Leah or her son, the only thing we do know is that he married and bore at least one son who inherited Tara. Perhaps his journals will shed some light on what happened to his mother."

Addressing the others, Grandmother handed me what we now assumed from the dates was the last diary kept, "Since Lucy has read all of her great-great-grandmother's diaries, I think she should be the one to read this one."

Everyone nodded their heads in agreement as Grandmother split the remaining diaries up between the remainder of the group.

Cieran was the first to leave as he went back to the stables to take care of the horses promising to read the diaries in his possession. Mom was quickly off downstairs, tucking her assigned diaries into her over-sized purse, to meet Dad for a quick lunch in the kitchen leaving Grandmother and I sitting in silence until she finally asked,

"Fancy a .walk around the gardens to clear the cobwebs?"

Just nodding, I followed her into the hall where we were quickly joined by Guinevere and Lancelot. As we strolled through the grounds, Grandmother suddenly stopped and turning me to face her asked, "Are you really happy here Lucy?"

The pained expression in her eyes caused a cry to catch in my throat as I grabbed her in a tight hug and tried to make light of all the problems, "Of course I am Grandmother, aside from the attempted drowning and choking by a murderous spirit, everything is great. Seriously though, once we solve this mystery everything will be perfect and I do love Tara and having the whole family here. John's behavior appears to be becoming more and more violent so if your theory is right and the spirit of John is away in Dublin, I think we need to get busy reading those diaries before he returns again."

Chapter 16

I feared this would happen. John has returned from Dublin just in time for the Christmas Ball in a vile temper. Last night, he returned drunk after gaming with his friends, locked Guinevere and Lancelot out of the house and forced his way into my bedchamber. Again he accused me of all manner of disgusting things and threatened to keep my beloved son from me again this Christmas. He laughed and mocked me when he told me that for the last three years he has gone to see our son alone and when the poor child begged to come home for Christmas, he told him that it was all down to me and I didn't want him here.

I can take this no more. I fear my beloved son is lost to me forever. I must somehow flee this house.

Slamming the diary shut, I swore under my breath, "What a rotten bastard!" before heading downstairs with the diary to the kitchen for a soothing cup of tea. That's where I found Grandmother. She never heard me enter as she sat there teary eyed, staring off into the distance, Leah's son's open diary in front of her.

"Grandmother, are you alright?"

Brushing away a tear that had escaped her eye and rolled down her check, she smiled weakly,

"Yes, but I have just read the saddest, most shocking thing."

Sliding in across from her and pouring myself a cup of tea from the cozy covered pot, "You and me both. You go first."

"It seems your great-great grandfather did bring his son home for Christmas but when the poor child arrived on Christmas Eve and ran up the stairs to his mother's room, she wasn't there. His father told him that she had grown tired of being a wife and mother and had just run away, disappearing into the night. The child blamed himself for causing the breakup of the family."

Remembering how I had felt about my parent's separation just months before, I could feel nothing but sympathy for the poor boy.

Opening Great-Great Grandmother Leah's diary to the page I had marked, I laid it on the table in front of Grandmother. Putting on her reading glasses again, she scanned the page before turning her attention back to me, "As soon as we finish our tea, we need to read on and see if Leah discloses any more details of her plan to escape and if she mentions Mr. Collier again. I have a strong feeling that his murder is directly linked to her escape attempt."

We had just finished our tea and were ready to head back to the library when Cieran appeared at the kitchen door carrying the diaries he had been given to read. "Mrs. Lacy, there weren't any new clues about what happened to my great-great grandfather or Leah in any of her son's diaries you gave me. The main theme of them seemed to be that he never quite believed what his father had told him about his mother going away. He referred to his mother as his 'beautiful angel'. Perhaps, he also believed she had been murdered."

"Perhaps, Lucy and I were just going back up to the library to finish Lucy's last diary. Can I get you a cup of tea before I go?

"I can manage, but thank you, Mrs. Lacy. Where's Miss Maude today?"

"She just went down the village to see if her mother might recall any stories that may have been passed down through the family. Her family has worked at Tara nearly as long as yours have, you know."

Chuckling quietly as he flashed a smile in my direction, he said, "How's the Christmas decorating going? Have you had time to do anything with everything else going on?"

"It's coming along. We'll need the tree for the hall brought in tomorrow when you have time."

Turning on his heel, Cieran headed for the door calling back over his shoulder, "Will do, Mrs. Lacy. Just let me know what time you'll be ready for it. We have it already cut and sitting in a bucket of water in the barn keeping it fresh."

Grandmother and I had just settled in our armchairs in front of the fire with Guinevere and Lancelot at our feet, when familiar footsteps approached the library door. Without even looking up from the diary she was reading Grandmother called, "Come in, Maude."

Maude was red-faced and out of breath when she entered the library, "Sorry I wasn't here to get your tea, Mrs. Lacy but once Mother gets to talking about the old days, it's hard to get away."

"It's no problem at all. How was your mother today? I hope she is well. Was she able to help with our mystery?"

"Well, I'm not sure since everything happened before her time here at the house, but she seems to recall that there was talk that Mistress Leah disappeared either the night of the Christmas Ball or the next day. She says she remembers distinctly that the whole village turned out to look for Mistress Leah on Christmas Day. She also seemed to vaguely remember something about a fire about the same time and workmen brought in from Dublin to repair the damage. But to be

126

honest ma'am, she seemed very confused today so I'm not sure if what she says is true or if it's her mind playing tricks on her."

"Please thank your mother for us and be sure that she knows that we expect to see her here over Christmas."

"I will. Thank you, Ma'am. She is looking forward to it," replied Maude as she gathered up the tea tray and headed back to the kitchen.

Without saying a word, Grandmother stood and strode out into the hall, with Guinevere and Lancelot on her heels. Before I could manage to get out of my chair she had exited the front door and was heading down the steps and across the drive in the directions of the stables.

"Grandmother, where are you going?"

Turning back she motioned me to follow her and shouted, "We need to tell Cieran what we have just learned."

Chapter 17

Now that the date for Leah's disappearance had been narrowed down to either December 23, the night that a Christmas Ball was held here at Tara, or the day after, according to the household ledgers and Maude's mother's recollections, Cieran was eager to discover if his great-great grandfather died about the same time.

It was dusk before Cieran had time from his duties at the stables to make his way to the graveyard. Most of the engraving on the old stones had been worn away by the wind and rain and what was still left was covered by the ever-encroaching ivy. Crouching down in front of the stone, Cieran cleared away the ivy from the stone and brushed away as much dirt as possible. He had taken the paper and charcoal, as Mrs. Lacy had suggested, trying to try to trace the date of his great-great grandfather's death. Just as he began pressing the paper against the cold stone and rubbing he was struck from behind and everything suddenly faded to black.

It was the feeling of being kissed that finally woke Cieran from the stupor brought on by the attack. Slowly forcing his eyes open, he found himself staring into the mournful eyes of Lancelot who continued to feverously lick his face as Guinevere stood guard over his prone body.

Struggling to sit up, Cieran looked around and finding himself laying against the boulders where his grandfather's body was rumored to have been found generations ago moaned, "How did I get here and what's that smell?"

As the wind shifted and the smell became stronger, the hounds began to howl as they turned and raced back towards home. The light from flames flickering over the treetops quickly caught his attention. Fearing the stable was on fire and the horses in danger; Cieran crawled onto his knees then struggled to his feet and stumbled through the now dark woods toward Tara. It isn't until he reached the clearing that the full horror of the situation hit him. Tara was ablaze.

Racing past the stables, he reached the smoke filled rose gardens. Barely able to make out the silhouettes of Michael, Patricia, Maud and Mrs. Lacy he yelled, "Where's Lucy?"

Lucy was nowhere in sight. Before he could call out again, Lucy burst through the patio doors, choking from the smoke and clutching her mother's portrait. It was the last thing Cieran saw before he collapsed at Mrs. Lacy's feet.

As I was being reprimanded by my parents for my stupidity in running into a burning building for something material, I hadn't noticed Grandmother on her knees cradling Cieran's head in her lap.

When the smoked shifted, I saw them, "Grandmother, what's happened?"

Holding up her hand that had been cradling Cieran's head, I saw the blood as she yelled, "Michael get Cieran's father, he's with the other men helping fight the fire and then take the car and go to the village for the doctor."

The fire was quickly extinguished and Mr. Collier carried Cieran into the sitting room in the undamaged wing of the house as we waited for the doctor to arrive. Maude brought hot, sweet tea for everyone to ward off the cold and shock as we waited to find out what had happened to Cieran.

Grandmother had already bathed and temporarily bandaged the gash on Cieran's head and was just attempting to revive him with her spirits of ammonia, when he suddenly opened his eyes wide and called out, "Where's Lucy?"

I quickly grabbed his hand and replied, "I'm right here Cieran," before his eyes closed and he faded into unconsciousness again.

Frantic, I cried, "Is he going to be alright, Grandmother?"

"Calm down Lucy. Cieran's had a bad knock on the head but I am sure he will be fine. He's a young, healthy boy. Until the doctor arrives, can you sit with him and continue applying the cold compresses to his forehead while I go check on the workmen and see where Guinevere and Lancelot have gotten off to?"

I sat quietly, bathing Cieran's forehead and talking to his motionless body until Dad arrived with the doctor. Shooing me from the room so he could undress his patient and examine him, the doctor went to work as I impatiently paced up and down outside the room.

It wasn't long before I could hear the muffled sound of Cieran's voice and burst into the room. What followed was rather embarrassing since Cieran was now wide awake and still completely naked. Clutching his scattered clothes to cover himself, the doctor quickly ushered me back out of the room. As the door shut in my face Cieran called, "We were right. It was John that killed my great-great grandfather and now I'm more than certain he killed Leah too."

By the time Mother and Grandmother returned, Cieran was feeling well enough to sit up and ready to tell us what happened to him in the graveyard. With the threat of the fire spreading now over, Maude had been busy in the kitchen and soon appeared announcing that a meal was waiting in the kitchen. As we all sat around the table eating, Cieran told us of being attacked in the graveyard and then waking up by the same boulders where his great-great grandfather's body was found those many generation before.

"Did you manage to get the date of his death from the grave stone before the attack?" Grandmother asked between bites of her ham sandwich.

Nodding, Cieran replied, "Yes, it was the night of December 23rd."

"The same night of the argument at the Christmas ball, and now this fire, could it all be related?"

The rest of the meal was spent with everyone calmly talking about the fire and making plans for getting the damage repaired. As for me, I was anything but calm.

Chapter 18

Thank goodness that Grandmother, always fearful of fire, had installed a sprinkler system years ago throughout Tara. With the help of every able-bodied man on the estate and the sprinkler system, the fire was confined to just one side of the library.

With his architect background, Grandmother asked Dad to supervise the builders as they went about repairing the damage done to the library by the mysterious fire, allowing her to finish preparing for Christmas.

Before dragging the workmen away from their work converting the stables, Dad asked Grandmother if she thought the plans for the library, added during the early days of John and Leah's marriage, might be stored somewhere in the attics.

We were just finishing breakfast early the next morning when Grandmother appeared at the dining room doorway, bearing a triumphant look on her face, "I found the original plans for the library. When you are finished your coffees we can look at them in the library."

By the time we drained the last of our coffee from the cups and walked to the still smoky smelling library Grandmother had already spread them out on the table in front of the fireplace.

As an architect, it only took Dad a few minutes to realize something wasn't quite right.

"Are you sure these are for this room, Maureen?

"Of course I am. Look, it says library, right here on the bottom, next to the date they were created.

"Well, according to these plans, this was a double fireplace room, with one on each side of the room.

I suddenly began to feel light-headed as the terrible scene between John and Leah during the Christmas Ball replayed like a movie in my brain. As I could feel my body begin to sway, Dad grabbed by arm and eased me into the closest chair as he asked, "Lucy, are you alright? You're not skipping meals again are you?"

"No Dad, for goodness sakes! I remembered something I think is important about the argument between John and Leah in this room."

Kneeling in front of my chair, Grandmother gently asked, "What is it that you've remembered?"

"Well, when I was watching the argument, I remember feeling the heat from the fireplace on my back."

Shaking his head, Dad interrupted, "Well, if the fire was lit, you would, wouldn't you."

Grandmother quickly hushed him, "Let the child finish, Michael. If she says it's important, it is!"

"Well, I saw John standing in front of the fireplace and I remember him throwing his drink in the fire and it flared up. I remember how frightened I was that the greens and other decorations on the mantle would catch fire."

Grandmother suddenly grew excited and turned to Dad, "Michael, I remember seeing old paintings and there was a fireplace on that wall. Could it have been covered over at some time, perhaps after another fire many years ago?"

Immediately, Dad began pulling away the scorched plaster walls, revealing a closed off fireplace behind them. As he continued to pull away the scorched wall he suddenly stopped and turned to Grandmother and asked, "Have you ever heard any legends about hidden stairways and tunnels here at Tara?

"No, not here at Tara, but I do remember reading somewhere that one local landowner had one installed during the early days of the rebellion. There were many big houses in Ireland burned to the ground during that time. But now that you mention it, it wouldn't surprise me in the least if the same fear may have gripped John during the famine. He did treat his tenants terribly. Why do you ask?"

Stepping aside, Dad pointed at what was obviously an old door and straining he finally managed to push it open wide enough for him to slip through.

Holding the door and staring into the blackness, Dad turned to me, "I'll need a torch, Lucy can you get one from the hall closet?"

Staring wide-eyed, I stammered, "Torch?"

Grandmother quickly explained, "Flashlight, darling. There should be one on the top shelf."

Racing out into the hall, I flung open the door and standing on tip-toes grabbed the flashlight and headed back to the library and handed it to my father.

"Lucy, can you manage to hold this door? It's quite heavy. Everyone else stand back. I'm going down these stairs and see where they lead."

The door was very heavy but by now my adrenalin was pumping, and I was able to easily manage to hold the door open as Dad squeezed through the opening and began his descent down the staircase.

Cobwebs hung from the ceiling of the stairwell and clung to Michael as he carefully made his way down the ancient, steep and slippery stone staircase. As he reached the bottom, the narrow hallway split into two separate corridors. Taking the corridor to the right he found a door and pushing it open found himself facing thick evergreen bushes.

Heading back to where the two corridors split, he called up to the library, "There are two separate corridors down here. The one to right leads outside to somewhere in the garden and appears to have been covered by heavy plantings. I'm going to follow the other one now. Be back in a minute."

Mom was wringing her hands by now as she called out to Dad, "For god's sake, be careful Michael!"

"I'll be fine, Patricia. Don't worry!" his echoing response came as Dad's voice faded off into the distance.

Everyone waited upstairs for what seemed like hours, holding our breath, as we waited to hear Dad report back his finding. We didn't have long to wait!

Chapter 19

"Patricia, you take over holding the door open and Lucy you run down to the stables and have Cieran come here with bolt cutters. I've found another door and it's locked. We'll need the bolt cutters if there is any chance of getting in there."

Mom grabbed the door as me and the hounds ran out of the library and took off running to the stables in search of Cieran. By the time I raced across the cobble stoned drive and found Cieran brushing down Dailtín, I was breathless. Looking up and seeing the look on my face, he dropped the brush and grabbing me by both arms, "What's happened? Is someone hurt?"

Gasping for air and unable to catch my breath, I quickly shook my head and blurted out, "Bolt cutters! Dad needs you to come to the library and bring bolt cutters. He's found a hidden door and staircase behind the burned wall. There's a locked door at the bottom of one of the corridors that runs off of the main hallway and he needs your help opening it."

Putting Dailtín back into his stall, Cieran ran to the tool room and grabbed the tool from the table and we raced back to the house. When we reached there, Grandmother had already retrieved another flashlight and handing it to Cieran, touched his arm, "Be very careful, those steps are very steep and the last thing we need is for you to slip and break a leg or worse."

Just nodding, Cieran grabbed the flashlight and with one backward glance towards me, called out, "Mr. Burke, I'm on my way down."

Dad's voice echoed back, "Be careful lad, there are cobwebs everywhere and those steps at the bottom are a bit wet and slippery, so go slowly. Whatever is in this room has been here for generations, so a few more minutes won't matter."

"Yes sir, coming down now. I'm almost at the bottom of the stairs now. I see two corridors, which one do I take?"

Swinging his flashlight around in an arc, Dad called out, "take the one to your left. Can you see my light?"

"Yes sir. Be right there."

Cieran had taken only a few more steps when his flashlight began to flicker off and on before going out completely and leaving him in the dark. Suddenly, he felt a rush of icy cold air taking his breath away. It felt like someone was slowly sucking on the air from his lungs as he struggled to more forward towards the light from Mr. Burke's flashlight.

After being attacked in the graveyard, Cieran quickly realized that the spirit of John Lacy was behind what was happening to him and for some reason it was him that didn't want the locked room disturbed. As he started to drift into unconsciousness, Cieran managed to call out as he threw the bolt cutters in Mr. Burke's direction, "John is here and he's trying to stop us! Open that door. Hurry sir!"

Grabbing the bolt cutters, he quickly broke the lock from the door and using his shoulder pushed it open. Not taking the time to even look inside, he quickly turned and raced back down the corridor in search of Cieran. It had only been a matter of minutes but the temperature in the corridor had returned to normal and Cieran was slowly struggling to his knees, his normal breathing restored.

Grabbing his arm and helping him to his feet, Michael shouted, "Are you alright?"

"I am now. Did you see what was in the room?"

"No, Cieran. I opened it and came back to you. We'll look together."

"I'm pretty sure I know what we'll find there If John didn't want us in there it can only be that he's hidden something there that he doesn't want us to find. It's either proof of his involvement in my great-great grandfather's murder and his wife's disappearance or..."

Wrinkling his brow as he stared into Cieran's wide eyes, Michael whispered, "Or?"

"Leah."

Turning and quickly making their way back to the now open door, they stopped at the doorway and stared. Cieran's theory had been right. There could be no doubt, the skeletal remains lying on the raised stone ledge was Leah. Lying on the floor beside her make-shift bed and covered with the dust of many decades lay a small leather suitcase. Being careful not to disturb the remains, Michael reached over and grabbing the suitcase turned and left the room with Cieran.

"We're coming up," called Dad.

Even before they spoke, we all knew instantly from the grim looks on Dad's and Cieran's faces that they had found her. Brushing off the dust and cobwebs as they made their way into the room, Dad turned to us and stated what we already knew, "We've found Leah's remains in the sealed room. I believe that the spirit of John attacked Cieran again trying to keep him from bringing me the bolt cutters. Once he managed to throw me the cutters and the door was opened, John's spirit suddenly disappeared. I have a feeling that now that Leah has been found we may have seen the last of his visitations."

Shaking her head, Grandmother sighed loudly, "If only that was true, but I have a feeling that there is still more to discover. What is that you're carrying?"

Laying the dusty suitcase on the table, Dad turned and explained, "We found this in the room with Leah."

Grabbing a cloth and wiping away the dust and grime, Grandmother slowly opened the suitcase. Underneath a few deteriorating items of clothing was another diary. Gently lifting the red leather book from the case, Grandmother pronounced, "Perhaps we will find the answers to our mystery in here."

Chapter 20

It was agreed that we would all meet up for dinner after Cieran finished his duties in the stables and read what we believed was the last diary of Leah Lacy.

When it came down to the time to read the last entries in Leah's diary, Grandmother handed the precious book to me, "It's only right that Lucy read her great-great grandmother's diary. After all, it was Lucy who Leah chose to help her."

No one said a word but everyone nodded their agreement as I opened the book and glanced over the words she had written before I began to read aloud.

"It appears that she began this diary right after the last one that described John's return from Dublin before the ball."

I can take this no more. John's temper has gone from bad to worse. Bad enough that he keeps my only precious child from me but he physically attacked me the night of the ball and worse yet, he has threatened Mr. Collier's livelihood and his very life itself. I am wracked with guilt that this good man's kindness to me has put him in imminent danger.

There is only one thing to do and I must flee this place. I will leave here with only my clothes and a few personal things and try to make my way back to my father's home and pray he will give me shelter and protection.

"He must have caught her," interrupted Mother in a hushed tone.

Everyone leaned forward in their seats as I turned the page and said, "There is more."

"It has all gone terribly wrong and now I fear these are the last words that I will write. Mr. Collier agreed to aid me in my escape and see me safely to my father's estate. I had planned on waiting until John was passed out from the drink and leave through the hidden door behind the book shelves in the library where I could make my way down the stairs to the door to the gardens where Mr. Collier would be waiting with horses. How was I to know that John had only pretended to be drunk and had instructed his manservant to spy on Mr. Collier? When I opened the door to the garden, it was John who was waiting for me. I was dragged back down the corridor and locked in this storeroom. I had been here for just a few hours when John's manservant, Collins, appeared bringing a tray of food and drink. He assured me that John meant me no harm and that he had admitted acting irrationally and would soon release me from this prison that now held me. As proof of his repentance, he had gone to bring our son home for Christmas. When I asked about Mr. Collier, I was told that unfortunately John had felt it necessary to dismiss him from Tara but given him a good reference so he could at least find another job. I was sorry to lose my only friend here but happy to hear that he had come to no physical harm at John's hands for trying to help me. He left

148

me then, saying he would return shortly for the tray. I wasn't hungry but very thirsty so I drank the wine from the glass on the tray. Within minutes the pains and nausea began. I have been poisoned and if I am correct I have very little time left. I now believe that Mr. Collier is in all likelihood dead and that John has left his manservant to do his dirty work and is far away from Tara so he cannot be implicated. If at some time in the future, some kind soul finds this diary, please tell my beloved son that I loved him very much and my last thoughts are of him.

A hush fell over the room as I gently closed the book and wiped a tear from my eye.

Dad was the first to break the silence as he asked Grandmother, "What do we do now?"

Reaching for the phone, she dialed, "First we have to notify the Garda. There has been a murder and we'll need them to have their team in to remove Leah from there and then we'll need to arrange for a funeral and proper burial."

It was ten days before Leah's remains was released for burial. The family all agreed that Leah should be buried beside her beloved son and so it was. The mystery had been solved and there had been no visitations from John or Leah until the day of the burial. We were walking back to the house and had just entered the gardens when I saw her. She was gliding up the stone staircase from the gardens towards Tara, dressed in the emerald green ball gown she wore in her portrait. As she reached for the door to the library, she turned, raised her hand in a greeting and smiled and was gone. Never to be seen again.

Epilogue

Five years have passed since I began my own diary, but I won't bore you with all my daily entries. I'm sure that you are far busier making your own memories.

Mom and Dad stayed with us at Tara until the barn conversion was completed. Father's career took off and he is now one of the most sought after portrait artists in Europe. Their marriage seems stronger now than ever and it's not unusual for me to see them walking hand-and-hand in the gardens like a couple of newlyweds.

Grandmother's health is still good and she still rides everyday but she no longer rides alone. Mother rides with her and between the two of them, four more horses have been added to the stables. Once a week, Mom goes to visit with Grandmother the brother she never knew existed and has formed a close bond with him.

As for me, I went away to Dublin and attended Trinity College getting my degree in literature. While I was away, I acquired a baby sister. Mom and Dad were both quite shocked but thrilled with the prospect of becoming parents again and little Maureen is the apple of everyone's eye, especially her grandmother.

I'm sure you're all wondering what happened to that deliciously handsome Cieran. Well, wonder no more! Two days after graduation, I married my best friend. I now spend my days writing mysteries and running the estate with Cieran by my side.

Lancelot went off two years ago to visit a suitable female and one of his son's came home to Tara. About the same time, Guinevere had, shall we say, a gentleman caller and she soon was delivered of 10 healthy puppies. Homes were found for all but the one female that I chose for myself. You see, the tradition continues, all ladies of Tara since the time of my Great-Great Grandmother Leah have had their own Lancelot and Guinevere and so will my own precious daughter.

Oh, didn't I mention? Cieran and I will be presenting my parents with their first granddaughter and grandmother her first great-granddaughter at Christmas. There are another five bedrooms on our floor at Tara and we plan on filling every one of them!

Everyone at Tara sends their love and very best wishes for a Happy Christmas or as Grandmother would say "*Nollaig shona dhaoibh!*"